DAWN LEE MCKENNA J

LAKE MORALITY

A *FORGOTTEN COAST* SUSPENSE NOVEL:
BOOK EIGHT

2018

A SWEET TEA PRESS PUBLICATION

First published in the United States by Sweet Tea Press

©2018 Dawn Lee McKenna. All rights reserved.

Edited by Debbie Maxwell Allen

Cover by Shayne Rutherford
wickedgoodbookcovers.com

Interior Design by Colleen Sheehan
wdrbookdesign.com

For Franklin County Sheriff AJ Smith
Thanks for the location that everyone will think I made up.
Truth is cooler than fiction.

CHAPTER
ONE

I n the Florida Panhandle, March is an unpredictable creature. Like a woman who's unsatisfied until she's tried on every outfit she owns, March is clear and warm one day, chilly and gray the next. On this day, the locals had been calling it unseasonably warm, even though March never had any idea which season it was in.

The baby gently kicked against the car seat, her feet too tiny and her knit booties too thick for the motions to make a sound. She stretched out one arm, reaching vaguely in the direction of the windshield up front. Through it, she could see the branches of the nearby palms bending in the breeze, as though they were waving to her.

The infant gave a half-smile, a little bubble popping at one corner of her mouth, as a set of keys landed on the driver's seat with an interesting jangle. Then she startled as the front door slammed shut.

She smiled up at the face that looked in at her through the back window, but the face didn't smile back. Then, suddenly, the face was gone. The little girl's eyes lingered on the window for a moment, until the movement of the trees again distracted her. She watched them for a bit, then her blue eyes darted back to the window, but the face was still gone.

The baby waited for a long time, until the quiet was too quiet and her pink and green sweater was too warm, and then she began to cry.

⚓   ⚓   ⚓

Lt. Maggie Redmond opened the door of her aging Cherokee and stepped out onto Market Street, which was, for all intents and purposes, the main drag of downtown Apalachicola. There were two streets between Market Street and Scipio Creek, which opened into Apalachicola Bay, and Maggie could smell just a hint of salt and fish on the westerly breeze.

Apalach enjoyed a fairly steady stream of tourists year-round, and the brick sidewalks of Market Street weren't busy, but they were respectably occupied. Beneath the green canopy of the Apalachicola Chocolate & Coffee Co., a few people ate gelato at the small metal tables or perused the day's offerings on the handwritten chalkboard.

Maggie was twenty minutes late for her 2:45 coffee, and she didn't need to check her watch to know it. Her neurological system told her she had about five minutes before she either face-planted or shot somebody. She yanked her long, dark brown hair into a makeshift bun, shut her door, and headed inside.

The shop had what Maggie would call a trendy, historical, hipster vibe without trying very hard. The brick walls of the turn-of-the-century building were hung with huge burlap sacks that had once held coffee beans, the ceilings were high and adorned with pipes that were there because they were always there, not because industrial chic was a thing.

There were cases on the left side of the room that held homemade gelato and handmade chocolates, but Maggie's vector was from the front door straight to the coffee counter by the back wall, where a huge, Byzantine contraption dispensed espresso like it was water from Lourdes.

As she headed that way, the owner, Kirk, came out of the kitchen, saw her, and went to wait behind the counter, his face a masterpiece of disinterest. Kirk's hair, a sandy brown mass that was graying here and there, was messily braided and topped with a multicolored beanie.

Underneath his apron was a Grateful Dead T-shirt that no doubt led strangers and tourists to think he was a lot more laid back than he was. Maggie had seen him smile only once, right after he'd thrown someone out of his store for being rude. Kirk's young wife was as beautiful and bubbly a creature as she'd ever met, and she considered this a puzzle of miraculous design.

"You're late," Kirk said when she'd reached the counter.

"So?"

"So now I gotta make it again."

Maggie felt a twinge of panic pinching at her stomach. "Where's the one you already made?"

"I drank it," Kirk answered impassively.

"What for?" Maggie snapped.

"Because I'm the only one who could, and that's way too much espresso to throw away." He spooned some beans into a grinder.

Maggie shifted her weight from one foot to the other and back again. "I would have drunk it."

"It would have been cold."

"It would have been ready," Maggie countered.

She watched him as he ground the beans, and tried not to lick her lips as the air in front of her became thick with the smell of the coffee's released oils.

"Is that the Hurricane Blend?" she asked. It was her favorite, a blend he'd spent months creating, and named Hurricane because Kirk said you had to hold onto something when you drank it.

He looked over at her wearily. "Yes, it's the Hurricane Blend," he answered.

She couldn't help a nervous swallow, and he gave her one of his most disdainful sighs.

"If you want your 2:45 coffee, be here by 2:45," he said. "Because, frankly, it's stressful for me when you come in here late, scratching and twitching like you just broke out of rehab."

Maggie chewed at the corner of her lip to keep from snapping out a rejoinder, or worse, a threat. As frequently happened, they were at an important juncture in their conversation, one that could end with her not having her coffee. They stared at each other a moment, Kirk with a measuring cup of grounds in his hand, and Maggie picking at her thumbnails.

"Go ahead," Kirk said, though whether he meant for her to go ahead and make a smart remark or go ahead and draw her Glock, she didn't know. "I'll let Spaz make your coffee."

Maggie swallowed hard as she glanced over at the chocolate counter, where a paunchy, balding, middle-aged man was meticulously transferring squares of fudge from a baking pan onto a display tray. His negative speed would suggest the flavor was nitroglycerine and peanut butter. The day Kirk had nicknamed the new hire Spaz was the day Maggie became afraid that she might actually like Kirk.

"That's okay," she said carefully. She looked back at Kirk and made herself smile.

"Don't do that," he said. "It wigs me out."

A few minutes later, Maggie climbed back into the Cherokee and left her door open while she took her first few gulps of coffee. Two extra shots of espresso and barely warmer than lukewarm, just like she liked it. Kirk's coffee made Starbuck's look like kids running a lemonade stand, which wasn't surprising given that he was a classically-trained chef who baked the bread for his small menu of sandwiches.

Maggie was about to reach over and pull her door shut when her dash-mounted radio came alive.

"Franklin to Franklin 103," said one of the dispatchers shared by the Sheriff's Office and Apalach PD. Maggie picked up and keyed her radio.

"Franklin 100 to Franklin, go ahead."

"Franklin to Franklin 103, we have a report of an infant in a locked car in the parking lot of the botanical gardens. Can you be 10-51 to that location? EMS will be on stand-by."

Maggie pulled her door shut and started her engine. "Franklin 103 to Franklin, I'm three blocks away, 10-51, 10-18 to the botanical gardens."

10-51 meant *en route* and 10-18 meant lights and sirens. Those might seem to be superfluous for a three-block ride, but they were meant to calm a frantic parent or alert a negligent one.

The botanical gardens were semi-attached to the Orman House Museum, though they were really a separate state park of their own. A combination of natural growth and careful plantings, they were a beautiful spot viewed by meandering along a looping path.

It was never packed there unless there was some kind of event, but today there was only one car in the small lot, a champagne-colored, late model Escalade.

A tall, middle-aged woman with a gray pageboy was standing next to the car, one hand holding a cell phone and the other patting at the back, driver's-side window.

The woman turned to watch Maggie pull in, and her face was flushed, her eyes wide with distress. Maggie knew her only by sight, but she knew that she was one of the volunteers who maintained the gardens.

Maggie's windows were open, and as soon as she cut the engine, she could hear a baby wailing from the car. It was the choking, frantic cry of an infant who had been crying for a while.

"I don't know how long the baby's been out here," the woman cried, as Maggie cut the engine and got out. "I can't find her mother anywhere!"

"So the mom's not just locked out of the car?" Maggie asked.

"No! The car's locked and the keys are right here on the driver's seat, but her mother is gone!"

Maggie keyed her radio. "Franklin 103 10-97 Botanical Gardens," she said distractedly, then hurriedly replaced her mic before rushing over to the car. She hadn't driven a patrol car in years, and no longer carried a Slim-Jim, though she'd never been all that good with one, anyway. Locked cars were usually an Apalach PD thing.

Maggie automatically glanced at the door locks to make sure they were indeed locked. They were, of course. "When was the last time you saw the mother with the baby?"

"I'm not sure, but they were halfway through the garden when I ran into them around one-thirty," the woman said. "I was side-dressing the tea roses with some coffee grounds."

Maggie looked through the back driver's-side window at the baby. She had no way to tell if the baby was red in the face from crying or from heat. It was only 75-degrees or so, but it would be hotter in the car. Maggie felt a flush of anger as she saw that not one window was cracked.

The little girl was wearing a light sweater over a pair of pink striped pants and a pale green shirt. Next to the car seat sat a quilted cotton diaper bag.

Maggie ran back over to the Cherokee, leaned through the open door, and keyed her mic. "Franklin 103 to Franklin."

"Go ahead, Franklin 103."

"Please have EMS en route to my location," Maggie said, and had the mic rehung before she heard the affirmative response.

She jogged over to the rock and oyster shell bed that edged the parking lot, picked up a rock the size of a small cantaloupe. She tested its heft on her way back to the SUV, then handed it to the woman before pulling her light hoodie over her head. She shook her tee shirt back down, took the rock back, and wrapped one corner of the thin hoodie around the rock.

She glanced over at the woman. "Move back just a bit, please."

The glass was safety glass, she knew, designed not to shatter. She didn't know how hard it would be to break, or whether she was risking broken glass reaching the back seat, but she did know that the baby had to come out.

Maggie tapped the corner of the front window too gently the first time, saw a crack with her second hit, and by the fourth hit, the crumpling window let loose, showering the driver's seat with hundreds of slightly green cubes. Maggie reached in and unlocked the door, opened it, and found the button to unlock all of the doors.

The baby had stopped crying, but was shaking with deep, full body hiccups. Maggie opened the back door, yanked the diaper bag out onto the asphalt, and was unbuckling the seat from its base when she heard the siren of the EMS van. It was hot in the car. It didn't seem deadly hot, but Maggie didn't trust her adult perception of it to give her an idea of the effect on a tiny baby who'd been closed up for a while.

"Is she okay?" the volunteer asked over her shoulder.

"I don't know. Back up, please."

Maggie pulled the seat out and set it on the ground. The sirens were just a couple blocks away, and Maggie thought maybe she should leave the child in her seat now that she was out of the car, but her maternal reflexes were faster than her cop logic, and she quickly unbuckled the baby and was pulling her to her own chest when the EMS van pulled up a few yards away.

Maggie turned in that direction as she held the baby, one hand behind her hot neck, and made soothing sounds into her ear. She only vaguely registered the woman behind her, who was fretting and talking nervously.

EMT Mike Owens jogged to Maggie with an orange kit in his hands.

"How long's the baby been in there?" he asked as he reached her.

"I'm not sure. Maybe as long as an hour."

"Hold her up for me."

Maggie pulled the child from her chest and turned her to face Mike, who quickly unbuttoned her sweater, then stuck a thermometer into her underarm and held her little arm down over it.

"Were all the windows shut?" he asked.

"Yeah."

"Parents?"

"No idea," Maggie said evenly.

Mike cursed softly, then pulled out the thermometer. "Her temps not bad," he said, reading the thermometer, "But we need to run her in and have her checked over just to be safe."

Maggie glanced over his shoulder as she saw one cruiser each from the Sheriff's Office and Apalach PD pull in. She knew she needed to look for the mother, talk to the volunteer, but she also felt a strong pull to go with the baby.

"Bring her to the van," Mike said over his shoulder as he headed back the way he'd come.

His partner, Victor Bloom, already had the back open. Maggie turned the baby back around and let her tuck her head into her shoulder, then followed Mike to the van as Deputy Dwight Schultz headed in their direction. He was skinny as a rail and quick on his feet, and got to the van before she did.

"Hey, Maggie," he said, his eyes cutting to the baby as his Adam's apple bobbed.

"Hey." She reluctantly let Mike take the baby from her and climb into the back of the van.

Richard Chase, the officer from PD, approached. Handsome in an unassuming way, and normally all smiles, Richard was one of Maggie's favorites, but he didn't look all that friendly at the moment.

"The mother was walking her around the gardens up until about an hour ago," Maggie said when he reached them. "Dwight, I need you to talk to this lady, get more details, get a description. Richard, can you search the gardens, the bathrooms, wherever, see if maybe she got sick, passed out, something…"

"You think that's what happened?" Richard asked her.

"Not really," Maggie said tightly. "The keys were lying on the front seat. And the doors were locked. But who knows."

"Well, hell, Maggie," Dwight said. "If you're gonna leave the kid, leave the kid, but you don't have to lock the damn door."

Maggie bit back a reply that would have more knee-jerk venom to it than facts to support it, yet.

"I'll check the bathroom first," Richard said as he hurried away, his cuffs and keys jangling.

Maggie watched a moment as Mike laid the now-quiet baby girl down on a gurney and started strapping her in. "Dwight, go ahead and talk to…this lady."

"Miss Herndon," he filled in for her. "She plays piano at my church."

Maggie wasn't surprised. Franklin was one of the least-populated counties in Florida. Only twenty-five hundred or so people lived in Apalach. Dwight was from Eastpoint, across the bridge, and its population was about the same. Around there, six degrees of separation would be an extravagance.

Maggie stepped closer to the back of the van as Dwight moved away. The metal floor was cool beneath her hand.

Mike looked up at her as he finished securing the baby. "You want to come?' he asked.

Maggie did. "I need to try to find somebody to notify," she said anyway. "But I'll come to Weems as soon as I'm done here."

She waited until Mike had pulled the doors shut and the van had headed out, then she walked back to the car. Dwight had Mrs. Herndon off to the side and was taking notes in his tablet as she talked. It looked like she had calmed down quite a bit.

Maggie squatted down next to the diaper bag, noticing as she did that the car had Franklin County plates. She unzipped the bag and rifled through it. There were diapers and wipes, some of those purees that came in a pouch, and a change of clothes for the baby. No wallet or anything else that might belong to the mother.

Maggie straightened up and went around to the passenger side, opened the front door, and popped the glove box. The registration was there in a vinyl folder. The owner was a woman named Kristen Morgan, and the address was in one of the gated communities in the Magnolia Bluff area of Eastpoint. They had some money, then.

Maggie pulled out her cell phone and tapped the number for the office.

Jake Porter, a thirty year-old deputy with thick black glasses answered the phone.

"Hey Jake," Maggie said. "It's Maggie."

"Hey, Maggie."

"You have a minute to run down some contact information for me?"

"Sure, what have you got?" Maggie heard papers rustling on his perpetually messy desk.

"I've got local plates and a car registration," Maggie said. She got out of the car, and walked to the back of the car to make sure the plate numbers on the registration matched the actual plate. "Registration says the owner is Kristen Morgan. K-r-i-s-t-e-n. Address is 2314 Grand Bay Drive."

"That's over in Turtle Cove," Jake said.

"Yeah," Maggie answered. She read the license plate off to him.

"You want us to contact?"

"Yeah. I've got a baby girl here in a locked car. Well, she's on her way to Weems."

"She okay?"

"They think so, but they took her in to check her out. If you get anybody, tell them to come over to Weems, would you? Then get back to me?"

"Sure thing."

Maggie hung up and walked over to where Dwight and Mrs. Herndon were talking.

Dwight stopped tapping and looked up at her. "So, Mrs. Herndon says the mom stopped and talked to her for a few minutes—"

"She seemed very nice!" Mrs. Herndon interrupted.

"—and that she seemed really nice," Dwight finished. "The best she can figure is that she saw them around one-thirty." Maggie nodded. Dwight looked down at his tablet. "About thirty-two, thirty-three maybe, strawberry blond hair, straight, in a ponytail. Green eyes, real pretty."

Maggie looked at Mrs. Herndon. "Any idea how tall she is?

"Like I told Dwight, she was a few inches taller than I am, so maybe five-six or so?"

"Okay, "Maggie said.

"Slim, she said," added.

"Yes, nice figure for having had a baby so recently," the woman said. "I noticed for that reason."

"What was she wearing?"

"I'm not sure about the pants. Light-colored, though. She had on a very pretty blue and white striped shirt, a button-down shirt. I have one a little like it."

"Okay," Maggie said again. "She looked back over at the car. The keys were still lying on the front seat. "How did she seem? What was her demeanor?"

"She seemed fine, I suppose, given that I don't know her," Mrs. Herndon answered. "She was quiet, soft-spoken, you know. We only talked for a moment. We said hello, and I remarked on the baby, such a cute little thing. She said some nice things about the garden, and then she asked where the restrooms were, and that was the last I spoke with her."

"Okay." Maggie sighed and looked over at Dwight. "I called the registration and plate in to Jake. He's going to try to contact a family member."

"Gotcha," Dwight said.

"Do you have what you need from Mrs. Herndon?"

"Yeah, reckon we're done," Dwight said.

The older lady frowned at him. "Oh, Dwight, please don't say 'reckon.'"

"Yes, ma'am," Dwight said apologetically.

"Thank you, Mrs. Herndon," Maggie said. "You can go back to what you were doing.

"Well, I was on my way home," the lady said. "That's how I found the car. I was walking home. I just live over on Avenue I."

Maggie nodded at her, and gently touched her arm at the elbow. "Well, thank you for your help. We appreciate it, and I'm sure the baby does, too."

Mrs. Herndon said her goodbyes, then Maggie and Dwight watched a moment as she headed across the small lot to Market Street.

"So what do you think's going on?" Dwight asked.

Maggie sighed and started back over to the car. Dwight followed.

"I don't know," Maggie said, as she snatched the keys from the front seat and went around to the trunk. "Like you said, if you wanted to leave your baby, why lock the door? I can see if she was running in to pay for gas or something, though she shouldn't be doing that, either. But not if she was just leaving her. And why leave the keys inside?"

"Another key fob, maybe?" Dwight asked.

Maggie popped the trunk. An expensive-looking stroller was folded up inside. On the other side of the trunk was a sandy beach blanket.

Maggie frowned over at Dwight. "Why not just leave her in the stroller back there in the garden?" Dwight shrugged at her. She looked out at Market Street. "Then just take the car," she added quietly.

"Car's buggin' you a little," Dwight stated.

"Car bugs me a lot," she answered.

They both heard gravel crunching behind them and saw Chase Richards on his way back to the parking lot. Alone.

"It just doesn't make sense," Maggie said. "If you're gonna lock the baby in the car and come right back, you just take the keys with you. If you're not coming back, you might as well leave it unlocked."

She sighed and stuck her hands on her hips. "I'm trying not to think like a mom here."

"How so?"

"I'm mad. At this woman."

Maggie's phone buzzed and she pulled it from her jeans pocket. It was an SO extension. "This is Maggie."

"Hey, Maggie, it's Jake. Got the landline for that address and the father was there. Craig Morgan."

"I don't suppose the mother was there, too," Maggie said.

"No. But he's on his way to Weems."

"Did you ask for her cell number?"

"Yeah, got it. I think it's off. Even tried to ping it. Nothing."

"Did you pull her driver's license, Jake?"

"Yeah, got it."

"Okay, send it out and put a BOLO out on her. She seems to have left on foot, so she can't be too far, but make it county-wide, just in case."

"On it."

Maggie hung up. She looked at Dwight. "Some women leave their kids for a boyfriend. Maybe she's with somebody that picked her up. I don't know."

"Reckon maybe the husband can tell you something," Dwight said.

"I'm hoping," Maggie answered.

Chase reached them and held up his hands. "Nothing," he said. "Place is empty."

"Did you check the Orman House?" Maggie asked.

"It's closed today."

Maggie sighed. "Okay, we've got a BOLO going out for the mother, Kristen Morgan. You guys should be getting her driver's license any second. Chase, can you and your guys start looking downtown?"

"Yeah, I got it," Chase said. "Are we charging her?"

"Yeah, I mean if she's over at the Soda Fountain getting a float, arrest her. Child endangerment."

"Gotcha," Chase said, and headed for his cruiser.

"You want me to go to Weems with you?" Dwight asked. They worked together frequently, as Maggie was training him for an investigator's position.

"No, you've got the robbery to work and the only crime we have so far is child endangerment," Maggie said. "This is just gonna get handed down to patrol, anyway. I mean, I was just nearby; it's not going to be my case. Probably not yours, either."

Maggie was one of two Criminal Investigators in the Sheriff's Office. Dwight would hopefully become the third. Maggie more or less handled things that carried sentences of thirty to life.

She shut the trunk and the doors of the car, then used the fob to lock it. "Go on back to the office. I'll catch you up later."

"Good enough," Dwight said. He shook his head slowly. "I just don't get leaving a baby like that."

Dwight and his wife had three small kids, and Dwight was as good a father as his wife could ask for.

"I know you don't," Maggie said quietly.

CHAPTER

TWO

Weems Memorial was as small a hospital as one would expect for the area. It had an ER and all of the other requisite departments, in miniature, but it was mostly used for the ER and things like setting bones and taking X-rays.

Maggie walked through the double doors of the ER. There were only two people waiting. The nurse manning the intake desk, Cassie something, looked up as Maggie approached the desk.

"Hey, Lieutenant," she said, smiling. "You here about the baby?"

"Yeah," Maggie answered, still in motion.

"Valerie's got her in exam room seven. Go on back."

Maggie was glad to hear that Valerie Broderick was on duty. She only knew her professionally, but Broderick was one of her favorite ER doctors.

Maggie knocked on the wall before pulling back the beige curtain and stepping into the exam room.

Dr. Broderick, her long, ash-blonde hair pulled up into a bun, was leaning against the rail of the bed, watching the monitor. On the other side of the bed, a nurse Maggie didn't know was leaning over the baby, talking softly to her as she taped up a clean diaper. The baby's color seemed normal, and she was calmly staring up at the young woman.

"Hey, Valerie," Maggie said.

The doctor smiled at her, but her heart wasn't in it. "Hey, Maggie. Is this one yours?"

"Yeah." Maggie stopped at the bed rail and smiled down at the baby, even though the baby wasn't looking. "How is she?"

"She'll be okay. She's a little overheated and probably a bit dehydrated, but her vitals are good," Broderick answered. "Either it wasn't very hot in there or she wasn't in there for very long."

Maggie was about to respond when there was some commotion in the hall, and then a man stepped around the curtain. His wide eyes only brushed over Maggie and Broderick before they fastened on the bed.

"Ellie?"

He rushed to the side of the bed as Maggie moved out of the way.

"Ellie?" the man asked again, though it wasn't really a question. He reached out as though to pick her up, then halted himself and laid a hand on her stomach. The baby refocused her attention to his face.

The man looked over at Broderick. "What's going on? Is she okay?"

"She's going to be just fine," Broderick answered, her voice smooth and reassuring without being sweet. "Are you her father?"

"Yes! The police called me!" He swung his head to look at Maggie, his eyes darting to the badge clipped to the front of her jeans. "What's going on? Is my wife here?"

"I'm sorry, sir, but can I see some identification?" Maggie asked politely.

"What? Yes." He took his hand from his daughter's stomach and pulled his wallet out of the back pocket of his cargo shorts. He opened it, then pushed it toward Maggie.

He was Craig Morgan, with the same address as was listed on the car registration. The photo showed him looking quite a bit more relaxed, but he had the same dark, red hair and green eyes. He looked to be the six feet and one hundred and seventy pounds that was listed.

Maggie nodded, and he closed the wallet, but didn't put it away. His eyes hadn't left Maggie's face. When she looked back up at him, she saw confusion and fear.

"Sir, we found your daughter in a locked vehicle at the botanical gardens. Your wife's vehicle."

"I don't understand," he replied. "Where's Kristen?"

"We don't know," Maggie answered. "Do you know where she was supposed to be?"

Morgan started to shake his head. "I—I don't...she said she needed to do some grocery shopping, and that she wanted to take Ellie to Lafayette Park or something first. It's been so nice the last couple of days, she wanted to get Ellie outside."

"When was the last time you spoke to your wife?"

Morgan started to answer, then closed his mouth and shook his head just a little, like he was trying to clear it.

"This morning, when I left," he answered. "Around 8:30 or so."

"And where did you go?" Maggie asked politely.

"We went diving for rock fish," he answered. "My sister Miranda and I. We just got back maybe an hour ago. Kris didn't say what time she was going shopping, so it didn't really seem...I mean, it didn't worry me that they weren't home yet."

He looked down at his brown sandals, took a deep breath and let it out again. Then he looked back up at Maggie. "Look, I don't understand what's going on. I need somebody to tell me something."

Maggie glanced over his shoulder at Dr. Broderick, who nodded just slightly.

"Sir?" Broderick asked. Morgan turned to look at her. "I want to give Ellie a little Pedialyte, try to hydrate her a bit, so if you'd like to talk outside..."

Morgan looked at his daughter, then back to Broderick. "But she's okay?"

"Yes, I think so."

Morgan hesitated, then looked at Maggie. "Okay, that might be best," he said quietly.

⚓ ⚓ ⚓

Maggie led Craig Morgan to a small waiting area meant for the family members of patients having surgery. It was empty, though the TV that hung from the ceiling in one corner was thoughtfully playing an afternoon talk show that Maggie didn't recognize.

She stepped over to one of the vending machines. Morgan looked around hesitantly, then sat in one of the upholstered chairs nearby. Maggie stuck her debit card in the machine and got two bottles of water, then sat down in a chair across from Morgan. He was staring at something over her shoulder.

"Mr. Morgan?" Maggie asked. He looked at her, then at the water she held out to him. He took it without looking like he wanted it.

"Thank you," he said quietly.

Maggie unscrewed the top on her water and took a sip, then set it down in her lap.

"Mr. Morgan, do you have any idea why your wife might leave your daughter this way?"

He looked at her, and rubbed hard at his chin before he answered. "I need you to understand, Kris loves Ellie. She's devoted to her, devoted."

"Okay," Maggie said gently.

"But, my wife has had some health issues," he said. He blew out a breath. "Mental health issues."

"What kind?"

"She's not crazy or anything," he answered. "She's bi-polar...and has some other issues."

Maggie felt a small pang of guilt. She had no experience with depression, but she did occasionally have some PTSD issues, and she knew that victims of depression hadn't brought their illness on themselves any more than she had her PTSD.

"I don't know much about bi-polar disorder," she said. "Can you explain to me what that meant for her?"

"When we first met, she was going on and off her medication. So, she would have these really high periods, you know, excited, optimistic, full of energy. That was actually what attracted me to her. I just thought that was the way she was." He opened his water, but didn't take a drink. "But then the lows would hit, and she'd be lethargic and depressed and crying; she'd think any ideas or plans she'd had when she was 'up' were just...stupid and doomed to fail."

"How long do these swings last?"

"Well, I mean, as far as I know she's been taking her meds. I haven't seen anything unusual." He took a drink, then shrugged. "She had some post-partum problems right after Ellie was born—"

"And when was that? How old is your daughter?"

"Almost four months." Maggie nodded, and he coughed quietly before he went on. "So, I mean, the meds keep things on an even keel, but she says they deaden her feelings, make her feel tired and just kind of blah." He held out a hand. "Not to where she can't drive or care for Ellie, you understand. She's perfectly coherent."

"Okay," Maggie said.

"But, what I mean is that she's seemed kind of down, but better."

"No highs, no lows?" Maggie asked.

"Right. I mean, I can't say for sure that she hasn't quit her meds recently, because she'd kind of seem the same, until it got really dark or really good." He shrugged. "As far as I know, she was taking them."

Maggie nodded her understanding. "Okay. But she might have gone off them, very recently."

"It's possible, yeah."

"If she was off her meds and going through a bad time, do you think it might make sense that she left Ellie there at the gardens?"

He opened his mouth to answer, then shut it and shook his head. She watched his eyes roam the room a moment before he spoke again.

"It's conceivable." He looked at her sharply. "But you have to understand, Ellie's everything to her."

"But when she was down, she could get really down, right? Talk to me more about that. You explained how she felt, but what did she do, how did she act when she had one of these dark times?"

Morgan sighed and rested his elbows on his knees. "Not too long after we were married—this was 2013— she actually started hinting that she wanted to die. That was the first time that I knew of that she had stopped taking her medication," he said. "But as far as I know, she never got that far down again, even the few times that she's quit again. She quits when she's in a manic period, a high. She thinks, she really believes, that she's actually just better, and that she doesn't need them anymore."

"So, you really can't be sure she didn't stop taking her medication," Maggie said gently.

He shrugged helplessly. "No, not with any certainty. She's been down, but not to a concerning degree."

"Do you have any idea where she might have gone? When she is down, are there any behaviors, any patterns? Things she does with any consistency?"

His eyes drifted away from hers, and he stared at a diabetes poster on the wall beside them.

"Mr. Morgan?" Maggie prompted.

He looked at her a moment before answering. "Like I said, she gets really down on herself when things get bad," he said reluctantly. He took another drink of water. "Year before last, before she got pregnant with Ellie, she quit taking the meds. Things got pretty bad. She wouldn't even go see her therapist." He'd been looking her in the eye, but his gaze drifted again before he continued. "She cheated on me. Twice."

He looked back at Maggie, and she tried to look reassuring.

"She wasn't in love with them or anything, I mean, she probably wasn't even attracted to them. These were… not great guys. I doubt she even would have spoken to them under other circumstances. Once we were able to talk about it, once she went back to the doctor and got back on her medication, I understood that she was really just trying to punish herself. She thought they were all she deserved."

"As opposed to you?" Maggie asked gently.

"Well, as opposed to her real life, and yeah, us."

Maggie nodded, and gave him a moment. "But, you stayed together."

"Yeah." he answered quietly. "I love her. I understand… mostly…that when she's not on her meds, that's not the real Kris. She loves me. She wasn't trying to hurt me back then. She wasn't looking for something new. She was just…ill. Does that make sense?"

"It does," Maggie answered, though she wasn't sure she was big enough to have been that understanding. "So, if she was off her medication, if she was in a really dark place, could she have left Ellie because she didn't think she deserved her?"

It took Craig a moment to answer her. "I suppose. Yeah, maybe. But why not just leave in the middle of the night while Ellie was safe in bed?"

"Is impulse control something she has when she's like that?"

He shrugged. "No." He turned the water bottle in his hands a few times, watched the bubbles roll around. "But why leave her locked in the car? She knows that's dangerous."

"We probably won't know the answer to that question until we talk to her, Mr. Morgan," Maggie said.

"I know."

Maggie sighed. "When she does turn up, we're not going to have any choice but to charge her, but I'm sure between her doctor and your lawyer, you could get her some leniency."

"What will you charge her with?"

"Child endangerment."

He nodded slowly. "If someone had told me that she would ever be charged with something like that, I would have told them they were crazy."

"I'm sure," Maggie said, for something to say.

He nodded, looked down at the floor. "I'll be calling her doctor, anyway. I'll call my attorney, too, I guess." He looked back up at her. "Will you call me as soon as you find her?"

"I probably won't be handling this," Maggie answered. "I'm just here because I was first on the scene. But the

Sheriff's Office and Apalach PD are both looking for her now. As soon as they find her, someone with the Sheriff's Office will contact you."

He nodded. "Can we...can I go back in to my daughter, please?"

"Yes, of course," Maggie answered, standing. He was up before she was. She took his wife's key fob out of her pocket and handed it to him. "Here are your wife's keys."

"Thank you," he said distractedly.

She pulled one of her cards out of her ID case. "Please feel free to call me if I can answer any questions or be of any more help."

"Thank you," he said, reading her card. "I will."

Maggie watched him walk back down the hall and turn the corner toward the ER. Then she slid her ID into her back pocket, closed her water, and headed the same way.

THREE

Maggie had spent the rest of the afternoon helping the SO deputies and Apalach PD canvass the downtown area for the missing Kristen Morgan. No one had seen her, or remembered her if they had. Maggie had ended up going back to the far end of Market Street to talk to anyone nearby that might have seen the woman. There weren't many people to ask. Across from the gardens were several empty lots. About two blocks further north were the offices and public slips for Scipio Creek Marina. There were few people, and none that were helpful. The same was true for the Mill Pond, the commercial slips at the end of Market Street where all of the shrimp boats were kept.

After her fruitless interviews with anyone she came across at the Mill Pond, Maggie drove past the botanical gardens on her way back to the office. She noticed that someone had retrieved Kristen Morgan's car in the last hour. She had looked over there twice, half expecting to see Kristen sitting on the sidewalk, lost and wondering where she'd left her child.

After crossing the small downtown area, Maggie pulled onto the John Gorrie Bridge and headed across the bay to Eastpoint, where the Sheriff's Office was located. It was a five-minute drive across the water, then another few minutes to the SO. Maggie got there around five, an hour past the end of her loosely-structured shift.

She exchanged greetings with a few deputies on her way to her office, stopped to use the restroom, then sat down at her desk to file her report on Kristen Morgan. She was halfway through it when her recently-appointed new boss poked his head through her open doorway.

Curtis Bledsoe was a complete stranger from Orlando, a politician more than a law enforcement officer, who was apparently quite tight with the governor. He'd been appointed as the replacement for Wyatt Hamilton, the much-beloved Franklin County Sheriff for the previous eleven years, and Maggie's fiancé. Wyatt had chosen to become the SO's Public Liaison Officer so that he and Maggie could get married without either one of them losing their jobs.

Maggie looked up as Bledsoe rapped on her door jamb. It was his pretense of courtesy, since he never asked anyone if they were actually busy.

"What are you working on?" he asked instead.

Maggie tried not to sigh, or to focus on his meticulous strawberry-blond hair or his too-polished attire. He was always dressed for the desk, mainly because he rarely left it. Wyatt had been on the front line of everything; Bledsoe had yet to make an appearance there.

"I'm filing my report on the baby at the botanical gardens."

"What did that end up being about?"

Maggie shrugged slightly. "The baby is home with her father. We haven't located the mother."

"Well, that's not your job," he said simply.

"I realize that. I'm filing it because I was the responding officer."

"I know what responding officers do, Lt. Redmond. I'm simply asking you to finish it up and move on to your own case load."

Maggie imagined slamming his head in her desk drawer a few times. It had become a meditation of sorts for her.

"Yeah," she said, signifying little.

"Where's Deputy Schultz?"

"Last I talked to him was about an hour ago," she answered, turning back to her monitor. "He was heading back here to run those prints from the robbery."

Bledsoe yanked his head back and headed down the hallway toward the deputies' offices, the heels of his expensive shoes clacking against the tile. Maggie watched him, hoping he'd slip and fall on his round little butt.

Sadly, he didn't, though he did have to sidestep a little when Wyatt rounded the corner just ahead.

She smiled as Wyatt touched a finger to his SO ballcap in greeting. She heard Bledsoe issue some sort of greeting without bothering to look up. Wyatt was six-four, and Bledsoe no more than five-six. He didn't like to stand too close to Wyatt because it made him look as small as he was.

Maggie watched as Wyatt ambled toward her office, his strong build and lithe gait belying his almost fifty years. With his dimples, his moustache and his wavy brown hair, he was easily the most handsome man Maggie had ever known. He'd been a great boss, a better friend, and now in a couple of weeks he would be her husband. Maggie got kind of goofy about that when she thought about it.

Wyatt hiked up the thighs of his jeans and folded himself into the metal chair in front of her desk, then tried to arrange his impossibly long legs into a comfortable position.

"Hey," he said finally.

"Hey."

"Cap'n Crunch seems especially surly," he said. "Did they leave the kitten nuggets out of his happy meal again?"

"Who knows," Maggie said. "I wish somebody would run him over already."

"Be patient," Wyatt said. "Whatcha doing?"

"Filing my report on an abandoned baby." Maggie went back to tapping at her keyboard.

"I heard about that," Wyatt said. "Still no sign of the mom?"

"Nope," she answered. "According to her husband, she's had a really tough time with bi-polar disorder, so she may have just wandered off for a while. Regardless, this is not my case, as that twerp just pointed out, so I'm going to file this and go home."

"The baby's okay?"

"Yeah, her father took her home."

Wyatt nodded, then took his cap off and ran a hand through his thick hair. "So, are we still doing dinner at your place tonight?"

They'd taken to eating together most nights over the last couple of months. Recently, they'd done so at Maggie's more than at his place in town. Wyatt would be moving in with them, and he was, as he put it, "in transition."

"Yeah," she said. "Beef Stroganoff, if that's okay." She said it to be polite. Wyatt ate like an anaconda, and almost everything was okay, with the possible exception of almost every vegetable.

"Sounds good," he said. He slapped his cap back on his head. "Kids eating with us?"

"I think so," Maggie said. "I know Kyle is. It's a school night."

It was a school night for her daughter, Sky, too, but Sky was a senior. Kyle was only twelve.

"Good. I was thinking maybe some contract rummy after dinner," he said as he stood up.

"Only if you're good. You have to eat all your carrots," Maggie said.

"There are no carrots in beef Stroganoff," he said.

"There will be tonight."

"Well, then maybe I don't feel so much like cards."

Wyatt fiddled with some chipped Formica on the edge of her desk. "So, did you talk to the kids about tonight?"

Wyatt had spent the night at Maggie's a few times in the last few weeks, always sleeping on the couch. Tonight, he was sleeping in her bed for the first time. She was taking the couch. It was all part of their effort to get Wyatt more comfortable with the idea of living in the home she'd shared with her late ex-husband.

Even though she and David had been divorced for five years already when he'd died the year before, Maggie knew that Wyatt felt his presence there nearly as keenly as she and the kids did. Wyatt's place was a rental and the landlady loved him, but not the idea of having chickens in her back yard. Maggie had chickens, and wasn't giving them up.

They'd considered buying a house, but real estate in Apalach was dear, and they'd probably be paying the mortgage until both of them were dead.

They'd finally opted to delay the stress of that decision for a while, which left them with Maggie's place, which technically belonged to her father. Her grandfather had burned the mortgage on the property back in 1972. It was paid for, and paid for was within their budget.

"Yeah," Maggie answered. "They're fine with it. They think we're dorks because we're stressing about what they think every five minutes."

"We are dorks," Wyatt said. "But we're comfy with that."

"Yes."

Wyatt unfolded himself from the chair, glanced out to the hall, then leaned over and kissed the top of her head.

"I'm gonna run home and shower," he said. "I'll see you in a little bit."

"Okay," she said. She watched him leave her office, then turned back to her monitor.

FOUR

Maggie put the Jeep in neutral and pulled the mail out of her mailbox before continuing on down the dirt road that led to her home.

The property was five acres that had a good-sized creek to one side and the Apalachicola River at its back. The cypress stilt house that her grandfather had built in the fifties sat almost squarely in the middle, surrounded by old growth oaks and pines.

Maggie had grown up in her parents' home on the bay, but she'd lived in her little house in the woods since she and her late ex-husband David had gotten married in 1998. It was home.

There were two vehicles in the gravel parking area in front of the house: Wyatt's huge Chevy pickup and the old Ford Ranger that had been David's. It was Sky's now, and she treated it like a brand-new truck.

By the time Maggie had parked next to Wyatt and shut off the Cherokee, her dog Coco, a portly half-Lab, half-Catahoula, had slammed out of the screen door and was hurtling down the deck stairs.

She hit the ground about the same time as Maggie got out of the Jeep, and Maggie met her halfway to the house. Her rooster, Stoopid, usually raced Coco to the car, but he was nowhere to be seen.

This was becoming more frequent, since he had, in the last several months, managed to turn himself into a house rooster. Maggie used to kick him out several times a day. Now, he spent most of his time inside. "Hey, baby," Maggie cooed, as Coco vibrated at her feet, her tags jangling.

Maggie rubbed the dog's neck as she looked toward the raised bed garden area, and the chicken yard beyond it. No sign of Stoopid.

"Come on, baby," Maggie said, and she headed up the wooden stairs, Coco at her heels. She was halfway up the stairs when Stoopid appeared through the screen door, yammering excitedly about unknown things of exceptional importance.

"Hey, Stoopid," Maggie said as she opened the screen door.

Stoopid reluctantly backed up just enough to let Maggie and Coco through the door, and Maggie let it slap shut behind her, as she put her purse and the mail down on the well-worn dining room table that her grandfather had built himself, from trees he'd cut from his own property.

Wyatt was sitting on the couch with his back to her, watching the news. "Hey," he said without turning.

"Hey," Maggie answered. She took her badge and weapon from her belt and set them down next to her purse. Then she tried not to trip over Stoopid as she walked over to the couch, leaned down, and kissed Wyatt's jaw. He reached up and ran a hand through her hair before she straightened up and walked into the small kitchen in an ell off the living room.

Stoopid was in hot pursuit, his polka-dotted diaper rustling, still giving her a rapid-fire report on his day, the state of the economy, or his imminent starvation. A few months back, Maggie had given in and bought him chicken diapers, something she only knew existed because her son had told her. Stoopid had spent the first couple of days falling over like he'd been shot, but after that he was okay. As okay as Stoopid was able to be.

Sky was at the stove, browning meatballs in a cast iron pan. Maggie looked at her with a now-familiar tightening in her stomach. Sky would be going off to college in five months, and even though Florida State was only a couple of hours away, it suddenly seemed like the other side of the world.

Sky looked over her shoulder at her mother. "Hey," she said. Her long dark hair, the same shade as Maggie's, was piled up in a messy bun that always managed to look professionally-styled. Maggie had never managed that effortless chic.

"Hey, sweetie," Maggie replied, as Stoopid let loose with one of his asthmatic crows. "What's his problem?"

"Wyatt turned Jeopardy off," Sky answered.

"Wyatt," Maggie said, raising her voice to be heard.

"He wasn't even answering the questions!" Wyatt called back.

Stoopid did have a penchant for Jeopardy. They assumed it was the theme song.

Maggie opened the fridge, and Stoopid's attention was quickly redirected. Maggie grabbed an RC for herself, and a couple of vegetable scraps from a bowl she kept for Stoopid. She dropped them into his cat bowl by the small butcher-block island and got him immediately off her case.

"How was your day, baby?" Maggie asked as she popped her soda open.

"It was okay," Sky answered. "I got a 96 on the death penalty debate."

"That's great," Maggie said, smiling. "What were the four points for?"

Sky sighed. "Apparently I sighed a couple of times."

"You'll train yourself out of that by your first court case," Maggie said.

Maggie had never planned to be a cop; she'd intend-ed to be a prosecutor, but the money for law school just hadn't been there. The fact that Sky had adopted her dream made her as proud as she was of anything. Sky qualified for a couple of grants and had applied for several scholarships, but it would still take a few loans to pay for Florida State. Maggie and Wyatt had agreed to worry about that later.

"Smells good," Maggie said as she went to stand behind Sky.

Sky pointed her spatula at the plate of sliced carrots on the counter. "Your man was whining about the carrots."

"He'll live," Maggie said. "Where's Kyle?"

"In his room. Homework."

"Okay."

Sky started transferring the meatballs to paper-towel lined plate. Maggie grabbed a fork from the silverware drawer and speared one, tapped some grease from it, and carried it into the living room with one hand beneath it. Wyatt was no longer on the couch.

She walked down the shadowed hall, waved at Kyle, who was doing homework on his bed. The bathroom door was open, the bathroom empty. She stopped in her doorway at the end of the hall and found Wyatt, looking huge in her smallish room as he sat on the edge of her bed.

"Hey," she said.

"Hey," he answered.

"What are you doing?"

Wyatt shrugged. "Just seeing how it felt."

Maggie smiled. "We're switching it out for your bed, remember?"

"I know," he said pleasantly. "What's that?"

Maggie moved into the room. "Meatball."

He opened his mouth like a huge baby bird, and she tucked it in. He raised his eyebrows appreciatively as he chewed.

"So how does it feel?" she asked him.

"Weird," he said after he'd swallowed. "Not as weird as last week, more than it will next week."

"You know, Sky suggested we switch rooms with her," Maggie said. "We could do that."

"I don't want to move her out of her room," Wyatt replied.

"She'll be moving to Tallahassee in August anyway," Maggie said. "She swears it's okay."

Wyatt nodded. "She's a good kid. But it's not necessary. It'll be fine. It would probably be a lot easier if you and David and I hadn't been friends for so long, but it'll be fine."

"I'm sorry," Maggie said quietly.

"Shut up," Wyatt said gently, and pulled her onto his lap. "I'm just gonna feel a little weird at first, that's all."

"I know," Maggie said. She tried half a smile. "I felt pretty weird kissing my boss for the first time, too."

"Yeah, but you got a lot out of that," Wyatt said.

Maggie laughed. "I did. But it was weird for a while."

Wyatt opened his mouth to say something, but Sky's voice intruded from behind the half-open door.

"Please don't be doing anything," she said.

"We're not; we're just talking about it," Wyatt replied.

"Well, could you stop?" Sky pushed the door all the way open.

"What do you need?" Maggie asked.

"Stoopid's doing his pterodactyl impression under the faucet again. I need you to get him out of the sink, so I can drain the pasta," Sky answered.

⚓　⚓　⚓

"Do you know why she just left the baby?" Sky asked.

They were sitting at the dining room table, halfway through dinner. Coco sat at Wyatt's feet, smiling up at him and trying to look like she just liked him. Stoopid was tapping around the perimeter, having a conversation with gravity about tossing him noodles from the sky.

Maggie shrugged. "Apparently she has some problems with depression."

Kyle looked up from his plate, a frown on his almost-pretty face. With his shiny black hair and long lashes, he looked so much like his father that Maggie and Sky sometimes felt he was still there.

"Why couldn't she just take her to a hospital or a church? Isn't that legal or something?"

"I don't know why, Kyle," Maggie answered. "She's the only one who knows the answer to that."

"Are you going to arrest her?" Kyle asked.

"It's not my case, baby," Maggie answered with another shrug.

"Mom has to be available for the next time somebody kills somebody," Sky said sarcastically.

It wasn't necessarily untrue.

They spent the rest of their evening in an easy quiet. The kids subjected themselves to a game of cards, then went their separate ways, and Wyatt and Maggie spent the rest of the evening watching a movie on Amazon and flirting with each other until they both realized it was starting to get really hard to stay the course they had, separately, set for themselves.

Wyatt was a preacher's kid who'd gone wild in his youth and come to regret it. He'd been on plenty of casual dates in the thirteen years since his wife's death, but nothing more serious than companionship. Maggie wasn't a preacher's kid, but she had been raised in church. Her ex-husband was the only man she'd ever been with, at least voluntarily. Their stance wasn't very popular anymore, but they were okay with that.

A few hours after she'd turned out the light and made herself comfortable on the couch, she was still trying to fall asleep. She was lying beneath her light blanket, feeling the breeze run from the river, through her living room windows, and on through the kitchen.

It was the kind of quiet that country people think of as silence and city people think of as a racket. The old oaks outside rustled noisily in the wind, and the crickets and frogs were working on their harmonies. Stoopid was roosting on the back of the couch, snoring quietly. To Maggie, it was a peaceful clamor, and she tried to let it lull her to sleep.

She was almost there when she heard the toilet flush, followed by a soft noise coming from the hall. Maggie was facing the hallway, and she waited until Wyatt appeared, in his sweatpants and tee shirt, doing the best sort of tiptoe that someone his size could do.

"I'm awake," she said quietly.

She watched his body jerk, and he looked in her direction as he muttered something under his breath. He placed a hand on his chest. "You scared the crap out of me," he said quietly.

"What are you doing up?" she asked.

"I had to pee," he said as he headed for the kitchen.

"We like to pee in the bathroom," she said.

"You're adorable," he said. "I went. Now I need something to drink."

Maggie heard him messing around in the fridge, then he reappeared with a bottle of water.

"Why are you awake?" he asked, as he made his way to the couch. Awake now, Stoopid started muttering like an old man.

"Shut up," Wyatt said without feeling. He held a hand out to Maggie and she took it, let him pull her upright.

Then he picked up her pillow, sat down, and plopped it into his lap. Maggie laid back down.

"I was having trouble falling asleep," Maggie said.

Wyatt stretched his legs and put his feet up on the coffee table. "What's twirling around in your mind?"

"Nothing," Maggie lied.

"Please," Wyatt said. "I heard you thinking down the hall."

Stoopid did a sideways shuffle along the back of the couch and started gently tapping at Wyatt's ear.

"Quit it, Stoopid," he said.

"Aw, come on. He loves you," Maggie said, smiling.

"No, he doesn't," Wyatt said as he waved the bird away. "He's looking for popcorn."

Stoopid fluffed himself up and settled back into his roosting position. Maggie sighed.

"I was thinking about the mom," she said.

"Okay," Wyatt prompted.

"I keep vacillating between wanting to punch her and feeling sorry for her."

Wyatt took a drink of his water. "Okay," he said again.

"If she wanted to leave the baby, she could have left her at home," Maggie said. "Or if this was some impulsive thing, she could have at least left the windows open and the doors unlocked."

"That's true."

Maggie sighed. "But then I think about her bi-polar," she said. "From the little bit of research I did at the office, going off meds, especially if it was suddenly, can lead some people to feeling suicidal."

"The husband say she'd ever tried to hurt herself?" Wyatt asked.

"He admitted that she's talked about it, but he didn't say anything about her actually trying to do it. But, he was trying so hard to make sure we didn't think too badly of her," she said. "He might have left something like that out."

"Maybe."

"So, maybe she was feeling suicidal. Maybe she's dead," Maggie said. "Maybe she was so distracted by what she was about to do that she didn't know the keys were in the car, maybe she locked the door as a reflex."

"That's a lot of maybes, but I know what you're saying,"

"So, I think about that and then I feel like crap," Maggie said quietly.

"Why?"

"Because my first instinct today was to find her, beat the crap out of her, and then stick her in jail," she said, her voice rising a bit. "And then I start thinking maybe she planned or plans to kill herself, and was trying to do the baby a favor, so I feel like a judgmental jerk."

"You're not judgmental." Wyatt argued.

"Come on, Wyatt."

"Look, you might be quick to jump to conclusions, maybe a little quick with the righteous indignation, especially when it comes to kids, but you step back and think straight after a minute."

"Sometimes," Maggie said.

"I haven't seen the exception yet," Wyatt said.

Maggie turned so she could take his water from him. She took a long drink, then handed it to him and laid back down.

"I've been thinking about Grace, too," she said quietly.

Wyatt nodded, like he'd already known. Grace Carpenter was a nineteen-year-old girl Maggie had tried to help the year before. A good and loving girl. She'd ended up jumping from the bridge. She'd been a strawberry blond, too.

"You have to look at every case from every angle," Wyatt said finally. "One of those angles is going to bring out some kind of emotion in you. That's how it works for all of us. We all have our weak points, the chinks in our armor. Yours is kids."

"What's yours?" Maggie asked.

"You," he answered after a moment.

Maggie spent the next two days helping Dwight with his robbery case, filing paperwork for upcoming court cases, and generally trying to stay busy so that she didn't worry too much about cases that weren't hers.

Kristen Morgan remained missing, and Craig Morgan called the SO at least three times a day looking for some kind of news. The case had become a missing person, given the length of time Kristen Morgan had been gone, but it still wasn't Maggie's case.

Three days after Kristen Morgan's disappearance, early Friday afternoon, Maggie and Dwight were having lunch at her favorite eatery, Lynn's Quality Oysters. It was a hole in the wall, run by oystermen and shrimpers who didn't care about ambience or new recipes. They served oysters and shrimp right off the boats, and customers had to walk through the oyster processing room to get to the deck in back.

It's complete lack of atmosphere *was* its atmosphere, and Maggie would have loved it even if they didn't serve the best oysters in town. The Sheriff's Office was only about a mile away, so Lynn's was a popular place for SO staff who were in Eastpoint at lunchtime.

"Amy's real excited about the wedding," Dwight was saying, as Maggie put just a touch of cocktail sauce on her oyster. "She's making her baked beans. Wyatt really likes her baked beans."

"He does," Maggie said before sliding the oyster into her mouth.

It was going to be an exceptionally simple and casual wedding. They were having it in her parent's back yard, right on the bay, and it was a potluck. They had only invited about a hundred people, and that included everybody's children. T

hey both wanted it to be the kind of party they would want to attend, and neither of them went for parties. As for the honeymoon, there really wouldn't be much of one. The department couldn't really spare them both at the same time, or maybe Little Lord Fauntleroy was just being spiteful.

Either way, they had a four-day weekend, which they would be spending at Wyatt's place, since he had the lease until the end of the month.

Dwight's Adam's apple danced around for a few seconds. "Did you, uh.... you invite Boudreaux?"

Dwight was the only person outside Wyatt and her family who would have asked that question. Bennett Boudreaux was the richest man in town, and a known criminal, though never convicted.

Last year, in the course of an investigation, Maggie had, inexplicably and against anybody's better judgement, developed an odd friendship with the man. He'd even saved her life once, and she his. He had become an important though problematic friend, and, as she found out late last year, he was also her biological father.

"I invited him," Maggie answered quietly.

"How'd Wyatt feel about that?"

"He didn't love it, but he understood it," she said. "In any event, Boudreaux declined. He didn't think it would be appropriate and he didn't want to...I don't know, make the day weird."

Dwight finished a steamed shrimp and nodded. "I can see how that might happen," he said.

Maggie was about to say something when her cell vibrated. It was the office.

"This is Maggie," she said.

"Maggie, it's Burt. Dispatch just went out, but they couldn't get you on the radio."

"What's up?" Maggie asked, already getting up from her bench.

"Found a body out at Lake Morality. A woman sorta matches the description of that missing woman."

Maggie felt a heaviness in her chest. "Okay. Dwight and I are at Lynn's. We're on our way."

Dwight had popped his last shrimp into his mouth as he got up.

"What's going on?"

"Body at Lake Morality," Maggie said, as Hank, one of the staff at Lynn's, headed their way with a pitcher of tea. "Might be Kristen Morgan."

"Aw, hellfire," Dwight said quietly, as he dropped a ten on the table.

Maggie held a hand up at Hank. "We have to go," she said. "Would you finish these oysters?"

"Gotcha," Hank answered.

"I'll be back later to pay, okay?"

"No problem, Maggie," he said. "Go on."

⚓ ⚓ ⚓

Nature and the State of Florida had colluded to make Lake Morality Road as desolate and depressing as it could be, primarily for the benefit of the prisoners on their way to Franklin Correctional.

Lake Morality Road ran off of Hwy 98, about two miles past Carrabelle. Once on it, it was hard to remember the pastel vacation rentals and glistening bay that had just been left behind.

Nothing adorned the road other than brush and unmotivated trees. It ran past Lake Morality itself, then through a couple more miles of this morose landscape before reaching the prison.

As a final touch, just in case there was anyone on the transport who was still clinging to a natural optimism, the road went on to dead-end at Tate's Hell Forest. Very few chipper prisoners arrived at Franklin Correctional.

Maggie took the turn off Lake Morality Road, which brought her around the small lake to the access road. Dwight was right behind her in his cruiser. The Cherokee rattled its way along the gravel through a small wood before delivering her to the clearing that edged a sandy launch.

It being just past noon on a Friday, and Lake Morality not being much of a hot spot anyway, there was only one civilian vehicle there, a battered, light-blue Silverado. It was flanked by two Sheriff's Office cruisers on one side and Medical Examiner Larry Davenport's van on the other. Maggie parked on the other side of the van, as Deputy Burt Simpson left a small group of people at the water's edge and headed toward her. He wasn't much taller than Maggie, had a good start on a middle-age paunch, and his reddish hair was starting to gray, but he'd been a deputy for almost twenty years and he knew what he was doing.

Maggie got out of the Jeep and met him half way, Dwight on her heels. "Hey, Burt."

"Hey."

"You have an ID?"

"Nothing on her, and she's been in there a little bit, but she looks like Kristen Morgan to me."

Maggie sighed and looked toward the edge of the lake, though her view of the body was blocked. "Crap."

"Yeah," Burt said quietly.

"So, she was in the water?" Maggie asked.

"Yeah. Couple guys from Sopchoppy found her." Burt shifted his weight a little uncomfortably. "One of the guys got snagged up and didn't wanna lose a new lure, so he went in after it."

Maggie looked around at the scene. "Anything to indicate she didn't drown?"

"Not so far, but Larry only beat you by a couple minutes."

"Okay, well let's have Mike tape the scene off anyway, just in case. We also want to keep out any YouTubers that might have a police radio. Can you get started on the guys' statements?"

"Okay."

Maggie started toward the launch, and Dwight fell into step with her. Her boots and his shoes crunched through the gravel. "I'm gonna talk to Larry and take a look at the body. Can you grab my kit?"

Maggie and Terry Doyle were the only two people with the SO who had any advanced crime scene and evidence collection training, and Maggie kept a battered red toolbox box in her Jeep at all times.

"Got it," Dwight said as he veered off to the right.

Two middle-aged men sat on a log, a good thirty feet away. Neither of them looked too good, and neither was looking at the lake. Maggie watched Burt as he started talking to them, tablet in hand.

Larry had two assistants with him. They were standing over Larry, who was crouching on the shore, but made way when they saw Maggie approaching.

"Hey, Larry."

Larry Davenport looked up at her. He was well over six feet, spindly of build, and well over seventy. His hair was almost purely white, but he had a full head of it. He was well past retirement, but he hadn't volunteered to and no one had asked yet. Until the 1990s, he'd kept up his practice and had been almost everybody's doctor, including Maggie's.

"Hello, Maggie," he said. "How've you been?" He had his arm up the front of the woman's shirt, taking the liver temperature.

Maggie nodded without answering as she averted her eyes and studied the upper body instead.

"The liver temperature isn't going to help us as much as we'd like, since she's been in the water," he said, "But once I get back to the office I'll factor in the water temp and try to give you a more specific TOD."

Maggie shoved a lock of hair from her eyes. "Do you have a less specific guess?"

"Oh yes," he answered pleasantly. "There's not been time for methane, carbon dioxide and hydrogen sulfide build-up, which is why she was still submerged—"

"So she wasn't weighed down or anything?"

"No, she wasn't," he answered. "I'd say she's been in the water four days at most, but judging by color and skin saturation, at least two."

Maggie nodded, but she was looking at the body, not Larry. The face was turned away, toward the water, but there was no doubt it was Kristen Morgan.

Her shoulder-length hair, clumped and tangled, was the same strawberry-blond shade, though the color wasn't as vibrant. Her blue and white-striped button-down shirt was twisted to the side and hiked up above her waist. With it, she had worn a white denim skirt that looked like it would hit just above the knee when Larry let it down.

"I'm pretty sure that this is a missing person," Maggie said. "She was last seen on Tuesday afternoon."

Dwight arrived with Maggie's toolbox. Maggie grabbed a pair of blue Latex gloves, then handed Dwight a pair. He started putting them on. Maggie squatted next to the body, waving at Dwight to do the same.

Larry looked up from his clipboard. "She hasn't been in the water since Tuesday. I'm certain. If it were January, then perhaps."

"Okay, Maggie said. "Any wounds?"

"Just this one, at least thus far." Larry turned the head toward Maggie. There was a bloodless, star-shaped cut just under her jaw. A fishhook, lure, and about three feet of fishing line were still attached.

"As you can see, there isn't much tearing," Larry continued. "The skin is still fairly resilient. So, I think Wednesday at the earliest, maybe even early yesterday."

Maggie reached toward the body, then stopped and raised her eyebrows at Larry.

"Go ahead," he said. "Mark got the *in situ* shots already."

Maggie gently pulled the woman's collar from the back of her neck as far as she could. There was no discoloration, no bruising that she could see. "It doesn't look like anyone held her down by the throat or neck."

"No," Larry mused. "Nothing on her arms, either. I'll check her more thoroughly when we get back, but I see no signs of restraint. Do you have any particular reason for suspecting something untoward?"

"Not really," Maggie murmured, as she stared at the fish hook jutting obscenely from such a delicate jaw. "Just trying to keep an open mind." She looked up at Larry. "Did anybody find any belongings?"

"Not that I know of," Larry answered, "But Burt was the first one here."

"Okay." Maggie said. She reached into first one, then the other of the woman's pockets, turning her gently with some help from Dwight. There was nothing there.

She stood up. "Dwight, I'm going to have a look around," she said. "Hang out here with Larry, okay?"

"Okay." He said, as she looked around the lake. The area to her right, where Burt was interviewing the fishermen, was open and clear, except for some sparse bushes. She decided to start with the area to her left, which was a shady area populated by a decent stand of pines.

It was easily five degrees cooler among the trees. A thick carpet of brown pine needles and pinecones made Maggie's steps almost silent, despite her hiking boots. She was only a few yards into the woods when she spotted them at the base of a tree.

The bright spots of color were a pale green leather purse, expensive-looking, sitting atop a neatly-folded blue sweater. Next to the sweater was a pair of white Keds, either fairly new or well-cared for.

Maggie squatted down and opened the purse. Inside was a red wallet, Michael Kors. Maggie opened it to find Kristen Morgan's now-familiar driver's license and several credit cards. Maggie rummaged gently through the rest of the purse's contents. A couple of tubes of lip balm, a baby rattle with a little stuffed lamb on it, a pack of gum, and a few receipts. Nothing like a note.

Maggie zipped the purse shut, took a few pictures on her phone, then set the purse aside to look at the sweater. There were no pockets. Maggie held it to her nose and caught the faint smell of fabric softener and something else. Not perfume or cologne, something softer. Maybe lotion.

Maggie put the sweater back and stood. She looked around her, but there was nothing else in the immediate area, save for a couple of Busch cans about ten feet away. They looked like they'd been out in the weather a while.

Maggie walked to the edge of the trees. Dwight was still hunkered down with Larry. Larry's assistants were headed that way with a gurney.

"Dwight," Maggie called. He looked over his shoulder at her. "Bring me three evidence bags. Large."

Dwight nodded and reached into her toolbox. A minute later, he found her back with Kristen Morgan's belongings.

"Those hers?" he asked as he handed her a bag slightly larger than a gallon-size freezer bag.

"Yeah. ID says Kristen Morgan," she said as she placed the shoes inside the bag.

Dwight squatted down, pulled a pen from his shirt pocket. "She leave a note or anything?"

"No." She took a second bag as Dwight labelled the first, and placed the purse inside. "No meds, either, but she might not carry them. They might be at the house. We'll check when we notify."

She handed the bag to Dwight , and while he labelled it, she bagged the sweater.

"What are your immediate thoughts, Dwight?"

"About her stuff?"

"Anything," she answered.

"Well, Larry says nothing right offhand says she didn't drown herself," he said. "But we're a good twenty-five miles from the botanical garden. If she wanted to drown herself, why didn't she just do it in Scipio Creek, or even jump off the bridge?"

Maggie got a sudden, but very familiar, picture of Grace Carpenter's body being pulled up onto a Coast Guard cutter, seaweed tangled in her hair.

"Right," Maggie said quietly.

She stood, and he followed suit. She waved at the ground around them. "No way to get any footprints with all these pine needles, but let's take a look at the sand between the body and here."

They started walking toward the clearing. "So, what else?" she asked Dwight.

"Well," he answered after a moment. "What I've read, drowning's not real uncommon in female suicides, but if she wanted to, she coulda just OD'ed herself on her meds, couldn't she?"

"Maybe. I don't know much about antidepressants."

"Well, we oughta check."

"Yes, we'll find out from her husband what she was taking."

They reached the point where pine needles gave way to sand and gravel. Unfortunately, it was mostly gravel. There looked to be a few partials, but they probably wouldn't tell them much. There were some depressions that could be from bare feet, but not clear enough to tell for sure.

"Hey, ask Burt to come get some pictures and casts of whatever footprints are here," she said.

"Okay, but some of 'ems us," he said, looking around.

"Yeah." Maggie watched as Kristen Morgan's body was transported to the van. "What else grabs you, Dwight?"

Dwight propped his free fist where his right hip would have been, if he'd had any. He blew out a breath and stared at the lake.

"How'd she get here?" Maggie asked after a moment.

Dwight looked at her. "You could walk it, if you had to, but it's been on the radio and in the paper and all. Seems like somebody woulda seen her, especially walking across the bridge. You don't see that a lot."

"Right," Maggie said. "Plus, would she really have risked walking along Hwy 98 in Eastpoint, right by her house? And if she was walking, and somebody picked her up, gave her a ride, you'd think they'd have come forward."

"Unless they didn't want to get involved," Dwight said. "Of course, once it gets out we found her here, I don't guess too many people would be feeling like admitting they dropped her off."

Maggie nodded. Dwight thought a minute, staring down at his shoes. "And then, you know, people party out here sometimes. You said the husband told you she cheated sometimes, when she got bad. Maybe she partied out here with somebody and drowned by accident. That would take care of how she got here, too."

"Maybe," Maggie answered. "Larry will do a toxicology. But I don't like it. Larry says she hasn't been in there since Tuesday. Wednesday at the earliest. So, yeah, maybe she was with somebody for a day or so, then they came out here, then she drowned accidentally because she was drunk or high, but it doesn't sit comfortably."

"I'm gonna run these to the cruiser, then I'll go get Burt on the footprints."

"Okay, Maggie said.

As she walked toward Larry, she watched as the gurney was secured in the back of the van and the back doors were shut. Larry stood nearby, talking on his cell. He hung up when she was still a few yards away.

"I'll give you a call in a few hours, Maggie," he said. "I should have at least a little bit more to tell you by then. Once I open her up, take a look at her lungs."

"Will you run a toxicology?"

"Of course," Larry said. "Protocol."

Maggie nodded, looked over at the lake.

"I can't think of a more depressing place to die," she said quietly.

Maggie and Dwight spent another hour on scene. Maggie talked to the fishermen herself, then let them go on home. Then she and Dwight took pictures, and collected every cigarette butt, beer can and candy wrapper they could find. Better to treat it as a crime scene unnecessarily than to find out it was a crime scene, but had been corrupted by a bunch of high schoolers skipping class to smoke pot.

Once they had everything they felt they needed, it was time to tell Craig Morgan that they'd found his wife, and that she was dead.

Notifying next of kin was Maggie's least favorite part of her job, and she tried to clear her head as she drove back to Eastpoint along Hwy 98.

There were stretches of the road where Maggie couldn't see the bay, and those made her feel closed in and out of sorts. She breathed more easily, relaxed her hands on the wheel, once the water came sparkling through the trees again.

Maggie signaled her right turn onto North Bayshore Drive, checked her mirror to make sure Dwight was still behind her, and reduced her speed. It was about two miles to the Morgan home on Grand Bay Drive, and she used the time to think about the questions she needed to ask the dead woman's husband.

The Magnolia Bluffs/Turtle Cove area was a collection of large, new homes situated on huge lots that were separated by stretches of skinny pines. The houses ranged from ordinary-large to ridiculous-large, and almost all of them were in a soulless style that Maggie thought of as Florida Contractor Fancy.

You didn't have to be rich to live in the area, but if you weren't, you were in debt up to your eyeballs.

The Morgan home turned out to be one of the smaller homes in the neighborhood, though it was easily three-thousand square feet. It was gray stucco, in that vaguely Mediterranean style that was so common in the parts of Florida that developers had built.

Maggie parked on the concrete driveway, a little way back from the open garage, where she saw Kristen's Escalade, a late model BMW sedan, and a new or close to new Chrysler 300 that had Duval County plates. Parked in the driveway was another Duval County vehicle, a Subaru Forrester.

Maggie got out of the Cherokee and waited for Dwight to park beside her and do the same. He had his tablet in hand, and hiked up his uniform pants as he walked over to her. He looked unhappy.

"Pretty fancy place," he said.

"Yeah."

"You're gonna do this, right?" he asked.

"Yeah," she said again.

They had only taken a couple of steps toward the front door when it opened. Craig Morgan stood there in khakis, a polo shirt, and bare feet. His expression was a mixture of hopefulness and dread, a combination Maggie always found terribly sad.

"You have news?" Morgan asked as they stepped onto the small brick patio in front of the door.

"Yes, sir," Maggie said. "Can we talk inside?"

"Of course."

Morgan swallowed hard before he stepped back and opened the door wider for them. They found themselves in a wide foyer, their boots echoing too loudly on the stone tiles.

It was largely an open floor plan, and Maggie ran her eyes around, to a study on her right, a formal living area to her left, and a great room and dining area up ahead. There were a few people seated at the large dining room table.

"We're in here," Morgan said, holding his hand out to vaguely indicate the direction of the dining area. They followed him there.

Along the way, Maggie noted the mostly new, contemporary, beach-house style furniture, and several framed pictures of the Morgans and of their baby girl. There was no expensive artwork as far as she could tell, there were no glaring indicators of wealth. It was an expensive home, but not a mansion by any means.

Craig Morgan preceded Maggie and Dwight into the dining area, where all eyes were turned their way; all eyes except for the baby girl being held by a woman in her sixties with striking gray hair.

Also seated at the table were a man and woman, both in their thirties. The woman wore her reddish-brown hair up in a ponytail and didn't seem to be wearing make-up, but she was extremely attractive. The man sitting to her left, at one end of the table, was dressed in business casual clothing. He had dark hair and wore glasses.

"Have you found my daughter?" the older woman holding Ellie asked, her voice an inch from desperation.

"Uh, this is Kris's mom, Kate," Morgan said. "And my sister Miranda and her husband Paul. Miranda's been staying with us off and on, to help Kris with the baby."

"I drove over from Jacksonville this morning," the man named Paul said.

Everyone but Kristen's mom was trying to fill up the space between her question and Maggie's answer.

Maggie saw it a lot, when people were afraid of what she'd come to say.

"May we sit down?" Maggie asked Morgan.

"Of course." He sat down at the other end of the table. Maggie and Dwight took the two chairs opposite Kristen's mother and sister-in-law.

"Have you found Kristen?" Morgan asked.

Maggie glanced over at Ellie as she started quietly babbling. Her grandmother gently patted her back, but her motions were fast, and her eyes were fixed widely on Maggie.

"I'm sorry, but we have," Maggie said to the table at large. "I'm very sorry to tell you that we found her body a couple of hours ago."

Craig Morgan just stared back at her, blinking. His sister gasped out an "oh no" before covering her mouth. But it was Kristen's mother who let out something between a cry and a groan. It was loud, and it was primal.

The woman pushed back her chair as she clutched Ellie more tightly to her. The baby started crying as her grandmother bent forward with another groan.

Morgan's sister jumped up. "Let me take her," she said quietly, and Maggie wasn't sure the woman noticed the baby being taken from her.

Maggie's eye was drawn to the wall behind Kate. In a wooden frame on the wall was a picture of Kristen Morgan, face covered in sweat but full of joy, as she held an obviously just-born Ellie. Maggie looked back at Morgan.

"I don't understand," he said, swallowing. "Where is she?"

"Her body's been taken to the medical examiner's office at Weems Memorial," Maggie answered. "But she was found at Lake Morality."

"I don't—I've never heard of it."

"It's not well-known," Maggie said. "It's a small lake on the other side of Carrabelle, on the road to Franklin Correctional."

"But…what was she doing all the way over there?"

"We don't know."

Kristen's mother had covered her face with her hands and was crying into her lap.

"How…uh…what happened?" Morgan asked, his voice breaking.

Maggie glanced over as she saw Kate sit up and focus on her.

"It appears to be that she drowned," she answered gently.

Kristen's mother started crying again. The sobs came from deep within her chest, and Maggie hurt for her.

"Maybe…are you sure it's her?" Morgan asked quietly.

Maggie looked back at him. "Yes. We'd like you to make a positive identification, of course, but her wallet and ID were there, and I saw her. It's your wife, Mr. Morgan," she said gently.

Morgan's eyes misted, and he looked from her to his little girl. His sister was standing by her chair, bouncing the baby and rubbing her little back.

"Do you know anything else?" Morgan's brother-in-law asked. "I mean, how'd she get there?"

"We don't know," Maggie answered. "We have a lot of questions, and that's one of them." She turned back to Craig, who was crying silently. "Mr. Morgan, she didn't have any medication with her."

"She always kept them with her, though." He cleared his throat quietly. "In case she wasn't home when it was time to take them."

"What was she taking?"

"Well, she took three medications. She was taking Abilify, Depakote and Xanax."

"Abilify," Maggie said. "That's an antipsychotic, isn't it?"

"Yes, but she's not psychotic," he answered quickly. "It's used to control her manic periods. The Depakote kind of balances that to keep her from going too low, either. The Xanax is for anxiety, and to help her sleep."

"Okay, I understand," Maggie said. Dwight was tapping rapidly into his tablet. "The times she stopped taking her medication, were you able to tell right away?"

"Well, not immediately, no. One time she just quit the Haldol. She didn't like the way it made her feel. Kind of stoned. But, I could usually tell something was wrong after a week or so, maybe less."

"Okay. Mr. Morgan, it appears that she drowned no earlier than Wednesday morning," she said carefully. She heard Kristen's mother take a deep breath. "I'm sure you were looking for her as much as we were, but can you think of anywhere she could have been for that long? A friend she might have stayed with?"

He shook his head quickly. "No. We don't even have any close friends here yet. We've only been here for about a year. We don't really see our neighbors. We have made some friends at church, but nobody we see very often otherwise."

"Okay," Maggie said. "Does she have a local doctor?"

"Not a therapist, no. We should have done that right away, but it kept getting put off," he answered. "We do have a family doctor here that gave us a couple of names. And a pediatrician."

"Could you get us the doctor's contact information before we leave?"

"Yes. Of course." He looked over at his mother in law. "I need to...do you mind?"

Maggie wasn't sure what he was asking, so she just nodded. Morgan got up and walked around a corner, behind a partial wall.

"What do we do now?" Miranda asked. "What do we need to do?"

"We'll need to ask each of you some questions, to help us try to understand how this happened."

"It could have been an accident!" Kate exclaimed. "She might not have meant to do anything!"

"That's true, ma'am," Maggie answered. "That's what we'll try to find out for you."

Morgan came back with a sweating bottle of water, unscrewed the cap, and held it out to Kate. She took it wordlessly, but set it down on the table.

"That's true, though," Morgan said as he sat down again. "It might have been completely unintentional. She might have just..." He shrugged. "She might have just thought she wanted to, but then it was too late. She wasn't a strong swimmer by any means."

"That's true," his mother-in-law said. "Kristen liked to be near the water, she liked the beach, but she wasn't much of a swimmer. We're from Ohio."

Maggie nodded. "We're not ready to make a decision yet," Maggie said. "There's no evidence yet that someone intentionally hurt her—"

"*Hurt* her?" Kate cried out. "No one would hurt my daughter. She was a very quiet and sometimes troubled girl, but she was kind and...she didn't make enemies."

"Mrs.—"

"Newell. Kate Newel. Kate." She was trembling, and Maggie knew that she was trying very hard to seem composed.

"Kate. I know that you all have had a very sudden and very shocking thing happen this afternoon," Maggie said. "You have questions now, and you'll have more later when you've had time to think. And I'm sorry to say it, but it's possible that not all of them will be answered."

Maggie looked at each of them in turn, couldn't help her eyes lingering the longest on the now calm baby who was resting her head on her aunt's shoulder. She ended up back at Morgan.

"Sir, it would be easier to talk to each of you alone, so that no one is distracted," she said quietly. "It'll also give each of you time to collect yourselves privately, to cry, to get some water. Whatever you need to do."

"Okay," he answered, nodding.

"Dwight, why don't you take—" she looked over at Miranda. "I'm sorry, what is your last name?"

"Cookson," she answered.

"Okay, Dwight can talk to each of you, and I'll talk to Kate and Craig."

"Would it be okay if Paul goes first?" Miranda asked. "I think Ellie's ready to be laid down."

"That might be best, ma'am," Dwight said, the first time he'd spoken since they got there.

Maggie looked at Kate as Miranda left the room. "Ma'am, would you like to lie down for a few minutes, or have some privacy? I'll talk to your son-in-law first."

"I don't want to lie down," she said. She looked lost for a moment. "I think I need to just go outside. I need to pray."

"Yes, ma'am," Maggie said. She watched the woman get up and test out her legs. Then Kate went out some sliding doors to a back patio. From where she sat, Maggie could just see the corner of a pool.

She looked over at Craig. "Is there somewhere else Deputy Schultz and your brother-in-law could talk?"

"We'll go into the den," Paul answered for him.

Maggie waited until the two men had left, then she turned to Craig Morgan as she pulled a small notepad and pen from her purse.

"You don't use a tablet?" he asked.

"No. I find I do better taking notes by hand," she answered. She was one of the few people she knew who didn't even have a Facebook account.

"Kris isn't much for technology, either," he said quietly.

"Mr. Morgan—" Maggie started.

"Please call me Craig," he interrupted.

"Craig. Tuesday, you said that your wife had talked about suicide in the past. Did she ever actually try to hurt herself?"

He swallowed hard, looked at a spot somewhere at the other end of the table. "She never tried to hurt herself that I know of, no," he answered. "She didn't even talk about it frequently or anything. Just a couple of times, when she was off her meds or when she was adjusting to new medication, that kind of thing."

"Okay," Maggie answered, scribbling in her notebook. She looked back up at him. "You said at the hospital that there had been infidelities—"

Craig looked at her quickly. "Wait! I forgave her for that! It wasn't her fault," he blurted. "I didn't drown my wife because she cheated on me a long time ago!"

"Mr. Morgan, that's not where I'm going with this," she reassured him quietly. "There's no evidence yet suggesting that *anyone* did anything to her. But, I do wonder how she got out to Lake Morality, or how she even knew about it. There aren't even many locals that use it. But, maybe she met someone who did." Maggie didn't mention that Kristen's wasn't the first body that had been recovered there.

"Okay. I'm sorry," he said.

"Can you tell me what happened?"

He took a deep breath and let it out slowly. "It was a few years ago. 2015. We went through a pretty bad time. I was pretty sure she was lying to me about taking her meds, that she was flushing them or throwing them away. She was angry with me that I wouldn't just accept what she told me. We…we just went through a time when we were fighting a lot. A little while later, once she was back on her medication, she sat me down one night and told me. About the—these other guys."

He scratched at his cheek, blinked at her a few times. "There were two guys that I knew about for sure. I mean, she told me that was it, and I accepted that after a while. I believe her. I don't think there were others. At first, I was just angry, and hurt. But after a while…I think it hurt her almost as much as it did me. She felt horrible about herself, for a long time."

"Okay. Can you tell me about these men?"

"They were not the type of people we hung out with," he continued. "She met both of them in bars. The same bar actually. A real dive on the other side of town. We were still in Cincinnati then."

"How do you know what they were like?"

He shrugged. "I guess I really don't," he said. "I never met them. But I did go to the bar once, about three months after I found out. I didn't go in; I just sat outside. But it looked like a pretty rough crowd."

Maggie nodded. She knew of a couple of places like that. She couldn't help wondering if Kristen Morgan had found her way to one of them. "As far as you know, this never happened again?"

"As far as I know." He rubbed at his face. "But she hasn't given me any reason to think so."

"All right. I didn't find a cell phone in her belongings, "Maggie said. "We tried to get a location on it several times after Ellie was found, but we think it was turned off. I assume you tried calling her."

"Yeah. Quite a few times. It went straight to voice mail."

"She might have dumped it intentionally when she left Ellie," Maggie said. "Or it might be in the lake."

"Okay," he said. He took a deep, ragged breath that seemed almost involuntary, then covered his face with his hands. Maggie waited a moment before speaking.

"I know you said she really hasn't made many friends here, but I would like to get those names. Is there anyone back home that she stayed in contact with?"

He put his hands on the table and looked at her.

"Yeah. Yeah, a few people. Uh, her best friend since high school, Kelly Lance. Mike Wallis, from college. He was like a brother to her. Um, she was still in touch with Sarah Gavin, I think. Sarah was our next-door neighbor back in Cincinnati."

"Can you give me their numbers? I'd like to see if she contacted any of them after she went missing. Or even soon before."

"Uh, Sarah's in my contacts. So is Kelly. But I don't have Mike's number. Kate might, though."

"I'll ask her," Maggie said.

Maggie pulled out her phone and used her thumbprint to open it. She pulled up a close-up of Kristen Morgan that Dwight had taken at the lake and then sent to her.

"Mr. Morgan, I'm sorry, but I'd like you to look at a picture," she said quietly.

He swallowed hard. "Of Kris?"

"Yes." Maggie waited a moment while he stared nervously at the back of her phone, then she turned it so he could see.

He stared at it for many seconds before speaking. "What happened to her face?" he asked, his voice barely above a whisper.

"A fish hook," she answered gently. "It was a couple of fishermen who found her."

He nodded, his eyes still on the image.

"This is your wife, though?" Maggie asked. He nodded, and Maggie closed her text app and put down her phone.

"Since this has turned out to be a homicide, someone from the Sheriff's Office will be coming by with a tow truck to take Kristen's car. We need to go over it, see if we can get any odd prints from it, or any other evidence."

Morgan nodded. "Okay."

"It should only be a couple of days, then they'll bring it back to you," Maggie said.

He nodded again, and they were silent for a moment. "Do you have kids?" he asked her.

"Yes. Two," she answered.

He shook his head. "I helped out with feeding and changing and all that, but it was Kris that knew every single thing about taking care of Ellie," he said quietly. "I don't—I have no idea how to be a single parent."

Ten minutes later, Maggie finished her interview with Craig Morgan. He'd given her the phone numbers she'd needed from his contact list, then said he needed to call his father. His mother had died of lung cancer while he was still in college. When Maggie had looked over her shoulder as she slid open the patio door, he was just sitting there, staring at the phone.

She'd found Kate Newell sitting on a low stucco wall on the other side of the pool. The older woman had stopped crying, but her eyes were red and swollen.

Maggie spent about twenty minutes with Kristen Morgan's mother. She'd learned that Kristen had indeed had a problem with post-partum depression after Ellie's birth. It was one of the reasons Craig's sister had come to stay with them, to help Kristen get enough rest as she learned how to be a mom. Kristen had been very grateful for it; according to Kate, Kristen and Miranda had gotten along very well.

Kristen's doctor had adjusted her medications to compensate, for the post-partum depression, though Kate didn't know what had been done, exactly. It had seemed to help.

According to Kate Newell, Craig and Kristen had been happy, their marriage strong. They'd been through the usual rough patches that all couples went through, but Craig had been tolerant and kind with Kristen, and Kristen was forgiving and flexible.

It was from Kate that Maggie learned that Craig had inherited some rental properties from his mother, added a few commercial and multi-family properties, and only in the last few years started making really good money.

Since moving to Florida, Craig had used revenue from his Ohio properties to purchase several commercial buildings in Franklin County, which he had fixed up to re-sell, often with owner financing. Neither family was wealthy, and everyone was proud of and grateful for his success, including Kristen. Her only complaint, a common one among young wives, was that Craig worked too much and too hard.

Kristen's mother didn't mention her daughter's infidelities, and Maggie didn't ask. If she didn't already know about them, she didn't need to learn about them today.

It was close to four by the time Maggie and Dwight left the house and walked to their vehicles. They stood there for several minutes while Dwight filled her in on his interviews with the Cooksons.

They were remodeling their house in Jacksonville, and that was part of the reason Miranda was staying with the Morgans. It helped the Morgans out, and Miranda didn't have to deal with construction. Paul Cookson was a general manager for Hilton in Jacksonville, and was able to stay in his hotel.

Paul Cookson was only there every other weekend, so didn't have much insight into the last few months in the Morgan home. He said the couple seemed exhausted with the late-night feedings and so on, but happy nonetheless. Miranda had said pretty much the same thing, and said that Kristen had been very tired, and sometimes overwhelmed, but not particularly down or upset. She'd never said anything to Miranda about being unhappy.

Maggie gave Dwight the phone numbers for the Morgans' doctor, their local acquaintances from church, and Kristen's friends back in Ohio. He was going to go back to the office and work on those contacts while Maggie filled out paperwork and waited for Larry Davenport to have some news for her.

Dwight opened his door, then hiked up his pants. "I've only ever had to be at one next of kin, and that was Axel," Dwight said. Axel Blackwell was Maggie's lifelong friend. His wife had been murdered back in November. "But I've known Axel all my life. I know how to talk to him. These people, they're strangers." He shook his head. "I'm hopin' you'll say it gets easier."

Maggie watched a gull as it flew over, headed for East Bay. "It doesn't really get easier, no. But you get better at it."

Dwight nodded. "I like the way you handle it," he said.

"Thanks." Maggie started for the Cherokee.

"Hey Mags?"

She opened her door and looked back at him. He looked enormously uncomfortable.

"Anything ever happens to me, I really need you to be the one that tells Amy, okay?"

Dwight was ten years her junior, but she'd known him most of his life. Maggie wanted to walk back over there and hug him tight.

"If you don't shut up, Dwight, I'm gonna have to go tell her right now," she said instead.

CHAPTER
SEVEN

Wyatt was in his office when Maggie got back to the SO. She leaned against the door jamb.

"Hey," she said.

He looked up quickly from his paperwork. "Hey."

He got up from his desk and headed over to her. She met him halfway. He was wearing dress pants and an SO polo shirt, his badge clipped to his belt. He only carried his weapon when he was called upon to fill in for one of the deputies or beef up one operation or another.

He glanced through the open door. Across the hall, the door to the office shared by several deputies was open, but no one was there. He gave Maggie a quick kiss to the temple.

"I heard you found the Mom," he said, frowning at her.

"Yeah."

"You okay?"

"Yeah," she said without enthusiasm.

Wyatt picked up a huge Mountain Dew, opened it as he leaned back against his desk. "You talk to the family?' he asked after a swallow.

"Yeah," Maggie said again. "Dwight and I."

She chewed at the corner of her lip as she stared at nothing on the wall behind his desk.

"What?" he asked, but it was more of a statement.

Maggie looked back at him and shook her head. "I don't know how she got there. I don't know why she left the keys and locked the car. I don't know where she was for twenty-four hours or more before she ended up in the lake."

"Anything saying someone put her there?"

"Not from the scene," she answered. "I'm waiting on Larry."

"What do you think?"

"I think none of it feels right," she said.

"But we are talking about someone who had some mental health issues," he said quietly. "Someone who might or might not be depressed enough to drown herself."

"In a lake that nobody but us has ever heard of," she said.

"People use the lake," he countered. "Mostly partiers and people up to no good. There was that stabbing over there a few years ago. But people know the lake is there."

"You know what I mean," Maggie said. "Locals. Locals know it's there. She's only been here a year. And it's more than twenty-five miles from where she left her car."

"I understand what you're saying," Wyatt said. "Just thinking with you." He took another swig of his soda.

"I know," Maggie said. "I'm just tense. I hate notifications. I hate unanswered questions."

Wyatt pulled his cap off, ran a hand through his hair. "You realize that if she killed herself, you'll probably never have answers for most of those questions."

"I know," she said again.

Wyatt opened his mouth to say something, but was interrupted when Sheriff Bledsoe piped up behind Maggie.

"Redmond, did you do the notification of next of kin?"

Maggie turned to look at him. He stood there holding a take-out coffee, his prim and proper silk tie loosened just slightly.

"Yes," she answered. "I just got back."

"I'll need that report by end of day," he said, like he didn't have time for the word 'the'. He glanced down at his watch.

"I'm getting ready to do that," Maggie replied.

Over Bledsoe's shoulder, Maggie saw Dwight, a drink tray of coffees in hand, go into the deputies' office. He rolled his eyes at Bledsoe's back as he sat down at the desk facing the hall.

"Do me a favor, Lieutenant, don't complicate things unnecessarily," Bledsoe said.

She looked back at him. "In what way?"

"You're a Criminal Investigator. You handle a lot of homicides. I get that," he said. "But the only reason you got called out on this is that we don't have cause of death yet. Try not to spend too much time looking for evidence that isn't there."

"You've been here long enough to know that Maggie's very good at what she does," Wyatt said quietly, his arms folded across his chest. Even across the room, leaning against his desk, he seemed to loom over Bledsoe. "She has no choice but to look at every angle until she knows what actually happened."

Bledsoe gave Wyatt a condescending smile. "I know how her job is done, Wyatt," he said. "I'm simply saying that there's no good to come of making more of it than it is. A suicide is bad enough, but it won't make too many headlines. We've got the boat show coming up, the Plein Air thing, whatever that is...we don't need rumors going around that we might have had a murder this week."

"I haven't said anything like that," Maggie said quietly. "I'm just doing my job."

"I'm not saying you have," Bledsoe said, trying to look conciliatory. "I'm just saying rumors start, and we don't need any rumors."

"Maggie doesn't start rumors," Wyatt said evenly. "Or fuel them."

Bledsoe held up a hand. "Look, you're her biggest fan. I get that—"

"I'd say the same thing about anyone else here," Wyatt interrupted. His voice was low, his face impassive, but Maggie would have backed up if she'd been Bledsoe. Of course, if she'd been Bledsoe, she would have rolled herself out onto a busy road.

"All I'm saying," Bledsoe said testily, "is that we need to be circumspect. Now, I've got to make some calls. I'll wait for your report, Redmond."

He held his coffee cup up when he saw Dwight at his desk. "Thanks for the coffee, Schultz," he said, then he was gone.

Dwight got up and came to Wyatt's doorway.

"Reckon I thought lye acted a little bit faster than that," he said.

"Better luck next time," Maggie said. She looked at her own watch, an old Timex she'd gotten for her sixteenth birthday. "See how many of those contacts you can get hold of before shift's over, okay?"

"Already on it," he said, and headed back across the hall.

Maggie turned back to Wyatt. He was staring at the floor, his arms still folded across his chest.

He looked up at her. "I have one year, four months, and some-odd days until early retirement. The day after that, I'm gonna drag Sheriff Bedsore out into the parking lot and whip his ass for him," he said.

"Good. But it's a felony."

"It's a felony to beat anybody's ass," he countered.

"It's felony-er if it's the sheriff."

"Please. Every person here will say he drew his weapon on me," Wyatt said.

"That's true," she said, and it was.

Everyone loved Wyatt. Everyone disliked Bledsoe. If loathing could kill somebody, he wouldn't be their problem anymore.

⚓ ⚓ ⚓

Maggie had just finished her report and was about to check on Dwight's progress when her extension rang. "Maggie," she said when she picked up.

"Hey, Maggie." It was their receptionist, Louann. "Larry Davenport's on line four."

"Thanks, Louann," Maggie said, and switched lines. "Hey, Larry."

"Hello, Maggie," Larry said. "I have some findings for you. I can give them to you over the phone, but I assume you want to come down here."

"Yep. I'll be there in ten minutes."

She grabbed her purse, dumped her phone in it, and headed out of her office. She stopped in Dwight's doorway. "Hey, I'm headed over to Larry's," she said. "I know you hate going over there and you've already had a rough day, so I'll go. I'd rather have you working those friends, anyway."

"Okay. I talked to that lady Sarah, but I haven't reached anybody else yet." Dwight took a sip of his coffee. "I just now got that fellow Mike's number, though, so I'm trying him next."

"Okay, I'll talk to you later," Maggie said. She walked the three steps across the hall to Wyatt's office, but he wasn't at his desk. She'd call him later.

CHAPTER

E I G H T

arry Davenport's office, otherwise known as the morgue, was tucked away at the back of Weems Memorial. Maggie parked in back and got out of the Cherokee. The wind had picked up considerably, and while it was warm enough, in the upper sixties, the air was thick with moisture and the sky was beginning to darken. They were in for some rain.

She found Larry in the autopsy room with Kristen Morgan.

"Hey, Larry," she said.

The old man glanced up from his clipboard, looking at her over his bifocals. He was almost as tall as Wyatt, but much slighter. With his white hair and his stooping posture, he always reminded Maggie of a really big egret.

"Hello, Maggie," he said.

Maggie walked to the other side of the stainless-steel table. Kristen was on her stomach, a sheet drawn up to her shoulders. Her face was turned toward Maggie. The fish hook had been removed from her jaw, leaving just a jagged, star-shaped wound, the flesh at the edges swollen with fluid. Her eyes were half open, but had long since begun clouding over with the cataracts of death.

"So, what is Kristen Morgan telling us?" she asked Larry.

"Well, of course, I haven't yet done a complete autopsy, but I do have a few important things to share, the most immediate of which is that I believe we have a homicide here," he said.

Maggie looked up at him, her heart rate taking a quick jump. "Homicide?"

"Sadly, yes," Larry said.

"Did she drown?" Maggie asked.

"She did, and I have confirmed that the water in her lungs is from the lake. It matches the sample we took at the scene."

"Okay," Maggie said.

"I've also narrowed down your time of death," he went on. "Between 8pm and midnight on Wednesday. I also have something for you to look at."

He pushed his bifocals up, then pulled the sheet down to Kristen's waist. Maggie immediately saw faint bruising on her back, two a couple of inches apart, and another, larger one centered about nine or ten inches below them.

"Tell me what you make of these bruises," Larry said.

"They're kind of weird," Maggie said. "Maybe someone hit her a couple of times?"

Larry nodded. "I thought perhaps the same thing," he said. "But when I played with the photos a bit they began to look like something else. Let me show you."

He flipped the first few pages of his report, then turned it around so she could see. The image took up the whole page. There were the three bruises, superimposed on the outline of a foot. The two upper bruises were in the ball of the foot, the larger bruise below at the heel.

"Someone kicked her?"

"No. I believe someone held her underwater with their foot. In shallow water. I found a good deal of sand in her mouth and throat." He coughed lightly into a fist. "Maybe they were trying to make it look like a suicide. Or maybe he just found this easier than holding her down with his hands. I don't know."

"That would still take a lot of force, though," Maggie said. "Does she have any fractured ribs?"

"No. But I have a theory that would explain both that and the fact that she has no bruising that would indicate restraints of any kind," Larry answered. "It will take a while longer for follicle testing to come back—those have to be done in Tallahassee, as you know—but her blood work shows quite a decent amount of chlordiazepoxide."

"What's that?"

"Librium. A pretty potent sedative," he answered. "Given her blood levels and its short metabolic life, I'd say she had quite a bit of it in the forty-eight or so hours prior to her death."

"That's not one of the medications she was taking," Maggie.

"Yes, I know," he said, flipping through his notes again. "Dwight called with her known meds: aripiprazole or Abilify, Depakote and Xanax."

"Would this have knocked her out? Was she unconscious when she went in the water?"

"Given a high enough dosage, it could," Larry answered. "Factoring in her weight and blood levels, I'd say it would have made her quite weak, and maybe given to periods of unconsciousness, but unfortunately, she was conscious when she went into the lake."

"How do you know?"

"Partly the amount of water in her lungs," he answered. "If she'd been unconscious, she would have taken in less. Also, I found skin cells underneath her nails that did not belong to her. She might not have been able to fight effectively, but she fought. It'll take weeks to match it to any DNA in the NDIS, of course, but if you have a suspect's DNA, we can match it quite quickly right here."

Maggie nodded. "Any other defensive wounds?"

"No, none."

"What about the medications she was on? Did they show up?" she asked. "Her husband thinks she might have been off her meds."

"That's a bit more difficult to determine until we get the follicle test back," Larry answered. "There were markers, metabolites, for all three, which we should expect given her long-term usage. However, the parent drug wasn't present. Now, those markers will only remain in the blood for three days to a week, depending on her metabolism, so she might have been taking them up until three days ago, but she also might not have."

"Great," Maggie said.

"Well, whether she was adhering to her medication or not, this wasn't a suicide," Larry said.

"Yeah, I know," Maggie said. "I'm just thinking about her state of mind, her behavior. Her husband said she engaged in some high-risk behaviors in the past, when she was off her meds. I was thinking maybe she was off her meds, and met someone who might have ended up killing her." She rubbed at her temple. "It's possible that she did leave her baby, and then ran afoul of someone a day or two later. Not probable, but I haven't had a chance to think it through yet."

"Well, this is what I have so far," Larry said as they both stared at Kristen's grayish face. "I'll be able to give you more once the autopsy is complete, and of course, let you know when follicle testing comes back.

Maggie's eyes drifted to Kristen's back, to the bruising just below her shoulder blades.

"I've heard that drowning is a terrifying way to die."

Larry took off his glasses and frowned at Kristen's body.

"Yes. I imagine it would be," he said quietly.

⚓ ⚓ ⚓

Maggie called both her boss and Dwight from the parking lot. Bledsoe sounded disappointed to hear that Maggie now had a murder case. Dwight just sounded sad.

Once she'd hung up, she'd driven out of the hospital intending to go straight home, but ended up at the botanical gardens instead. It was empty, but it was close to six. They'd been closed for some time.

Maggie wasn't sure what she was doing there. She blew out a breath and got out of the car, leaned against it for a moment as she looked toward the path where Kristen had spent her last afternoon with her child.

Everything bothered Maggie. Statistics said Craig Morgan killed his wife. She didn't know yet if Morgan had an alibi for the time of his wife's death, but he definitely had one for her disappearance. Dwight had verified with the charter captain that both Craig and his sister had been with him until almost three-thirty.

She pushed off from the Jeep as a thought started bouncing around her head. She grabbed her purse from the console and slung it over her shoulder. Then she pulled her keys out of the ignition, shut her door, and used the fob to lock the car. She stared at the back door a moment, recalling her days of hauling infants and toddlers around. She unlocked the back door and let a hand rest on the back seat.

You have Kyle in the stroller, she thought. *You put him in the car seat and get him buckled.* She looked at the back seat a moment. *Maybe you close the door, but probably not. You go load the stroller.* Maggie walked around back. Clicked the fob to unlock the gate. Lifted it up. Kristen wouldn't have had to do that, but Kristen drove a much-newer car. Maggie looked in at the small collection of items in her cargo area. Her crime scene kit. Kyle's cleats from last year. One of Coco's chew toys. An overnight bag from a weekend trip to Destin. It had been two weeks and she hadn't even taken it out of the car yet. The detritus of everyday life.

Okay, so you load the stroller, and close the trunk. Maggie pulled her gate down. *Your keys are still in your hand. Maybe you close the door,* she thought, as she walked back around the car. *Maybe you already did. Either way, your keys are in your hand.*

Maggie opened the driver's door. She stood there a moment, chewing one corner of her lip. She had her purse. Maggie ran a thumb along her purse strap for a moment, jingling the keys in her other hand. *You either toss the purse onto the passenger seat before you get in, or you get in and then put the purse over there,* she thought.

Maggie sighed, feeling a pang of guilt lodge in her chest. There was nothing that would cause her to keep her purse with her, yet toss the keys in the car. Unless someone was trying to take her and/or her car. Then, if she was thinking fast enough, she damn well would lock the doors with the fob, toss the keys on the seat, and slam the door shut. It would take maybe three or four seconds, if that. If she saw the person while they were still several feet away, looking threatening or maybe brandishing a weapon, she would have had time.

As far as the bad guy in question, the only thing that would prevent him or her from stopping Kristen physically was if they were about to need her death to look like a suicide.

She remembered how angry she'd felt toward a mother who might have left her child locked up in a hot car, and felt her face flush just a bit with guilt and embarrassment.

She got into the Jeep and dumped her purse on the seat beside her. She put the keys in the ignition, but didn't start the engine.

She found herself staring out the windshield at things that weren't there. She saw Kristen Morgan, her long hair splaying out like tentacles in the water, her arms thrashing for purchase that wasn't there, a foot on her back like she was a bug to be crushed. She could almost feel the woman's terror. She could feel the sharp, glassy texture of the sand as her face was pushed into bottom.

She could almost imagine that helpless, horrible feeling when Kristen knew she couldn't hold her breath anymore, that she was about to open herself to certain death. Did she have time to think about Ellie as the water rushed in and choked her? Did she have *too* much time to think about Ellie?

Maggie blinked away the warmth that threatened her eyes.

"I'm sorry," she said quietly, and started the car.

irst thing the following morning, Bledsoe called Maggie, Dwight, and Wyatt into the conference room for a quick summit on the Morgan case. They all had copies of Maggie and Dwight's reports, as well as Larry's initial findings.

Bledsoe sat at the end of the table beneath the picture window that looked out onto the training field. Maggie and Dwight took two of the seats to his left. Wyatt arranged himself up against the opposite wall, his copy of the case file in one hand, the latte Maggie had brought him in the other.

"Okay, so it looks like you two have your homicide case after all," Bledsoe started. "Schultz, have you worked a homicide yet?"

Maggie started to answer for Dwight, then checked herself.

"I helped Maggie with the Corzo case back in November," Dwight said.

"Right, yeah," Bledsoe said as he read from the file in front of him. "Another woman in the water. Ironic."

He flipped through a couple of pages as though to refresh his memory, then slapped his hands quietly against the desk.

"Okay. Redmond, where are you guys going with this from this point? The husband have an alibi for Wednesday night?"

"That's my first step today," Maggie answered. "Meanwhile, Dwight's going to pull his background and financials, just in case."

"Well, it's almost always sex, money, or both," he said agreeably. "Sex angle?"

"Not really. Not yet," Maggie answered. "She cheated on him a couple of years ago, but he swears he forgave her. From what I can tell by his demeanor, it's a non-issue. We'll see if we can come up with anything like an affair from his side."

"What's your first impression vis a vis motive?"

"I thought maybe kidnapping gone wrong, but there was no ransom call."

"Would the husband have told us if there was?" Bledsoe asked. It was a decent question.

"Maybe not. But, I don't think they have the money to pay a decent ransom."

"So, what are we thinking? Did she abandon her kid and then give someone a reason to kill her?"

"I have a theory about that," Maggie answered. "She was taken from the botanical gardens."

"Okay," he prompted.

"By all accounts, whether she was off her meds or not, she adored her child," Maggie said. "I honestly don't think she left her. I think she saved her."

"Carjacker that got pissed cause she threw the keys in?" Dwight asked.

"I thought of that, but what idiot takes on a kidnapping or murder charge to avoid one for theft? I think someone approached her with the intention of taking her. Maybe the car, too, maybe not. But I think yes, in which case locking the door and throwing the keys in would be the best thing she could do to protect her child."

Bledsoe stared at the wall over her head for a moment. "That makes sense," he said. "But now we need to know why."

"Yes."

"As we all know, it's almost always the spouse, so let's make sure we prioritize him," Bledsoe said. He closed the case file. "Okay, look. We're still seriously shorthanded. Coyle's still going to be out another week for his back." He looked at Maggie, then Dwight. "That means we have one and a half investigators for this. Dwight, hand the robbery case over to Shoemaker and Simpson. You're on this 100-percent. We're still three deputies short between vacations and Rupert's broken leg, so Wyatt, get the story about the Habitat for Humanity thing out of the way. Make sure they know we're gonna be volunteering our time in addition to the fundraising campaign."

"Okay," Wyatt said.

"Then get on this with Maggie and Dwight," Bledsoe continued. He looked at Maggie. "What's your approach going to be with the family?"

"You mean the homicide decision?"

"I do."

"I don't want to hit it straight on," Maggie answered. "I know sometimes it can be useful to put investigative pressure on a suspect, help them make a mistake or try to run. But, if he has something to do with it, and he runs, he's going to run with the baby."

"That seems sound," Bledsoe replied. "How do you want to split things up?"

Maggie was somewhat taken aback by his cooperative mood. She didn't look at Wyatt, but she was pretty sure he was, too. Civility was usually something saved for special occasions, like the presence of civilians or nuns.

"Well, if Wyatt's going to be available to help, he could help Dwight to run all of the background and financial data," Maggie said. "I need to alibi the family without scaring them, and get a medical release so I can talk to Kristen Morgan's therapist. I want to ask him about her medication and the effects of dropping it. I'm also hoping that Kristen talked to him about her marriage."

"All right," Bledsoe said, standing. "I need to be at the courthouse. Keep me apprised."

They all watched him walk out of the conference room.

"Just like old times, Boss," Dwight said enthusiastically once Bledsoe was gone.

"You guys have to stop calling me that," Wyatt said, pushing off from the wall.

"Sure," Dwight said.

"He kind of reminded me of a human being just now," Maggie said.

"Yeah, I don't like it," Wyatt said. "Probably some kind of ruse meant to lure us to our deaths, or at least some sort of ambush."

"Let's take it while we can get it," Maggie said.

"Wonder if it has something to do with the Mayor coming by yesterday," Dwight mused.

Maggie looked over at Wyatt. "Didn't you run into Van the other day?"

"Now that you mention it, I do remember that," Wyatt said. "He was out running around on Apalach 2."

Mayor Van Johnson, a sixty-something African-American with a gentle demeanor and a sharp wit, had license plates on his car, his golf cart, and his bicycle that read "Apalach 1, 2 and 3, respectively. Nobody ever saw him drive the car.

Wyatt," Maggie said, the promise of censure in her voice.

"What?" He shrugged. "He might have asked how things were going with the new sheriff. I might have said things were tense."

"The Mayor's over PD," Dwight said. "He doesn't really have any weight over here."

"Bledsoe's a politician. The Mayor's a politician. Bledsoe sucks up to all of them."

"Aw, I wouldn't call Van a politician," Dwight said defensively.

"He's been elected mayor one hundred and twenty-two times," Wyatt said as he tossed his empty cup in the trash. "Besides, I didn't mean it as an insult. I'm crazy about the guy."

"Forget about Bledsoe," Maggie said. "Let's just try to figure out who killed Kristen, before we have to tell her husband that somebody did."

⚓   ⚓   ⚓

Maggie was relieved to find everyone present at the Morgan home. The family vehicles were parked in the same places they had been the day before, and Maggie parked behind the Forrester. Someone must have heard her pull in, because Miranda opened the door just moments after Maggie knocked.

"Hello, Lt. Redmond," the woman said, clearly surprised.

"Hi, Mrs. Cookson," Maggie said. "May I come in? I need to speak with all of you."

"Sure. Of course."

Miranda opened the door wider. Craig was coming toward them when Maggie stepped inside.

"Has Kris's body been released?" he asked. "The man I spoke with yesterday said it wouldn't be till Monday."

"I'm sorry, I haven't heard when Dr. Davenport's releasing your wife's body," Maggie said as Miranda closed the door. "I'm actually here to talk to you about something else. You and your family."

"Uh, sure," Morgan said.

"Do you need my husband?" Miranda asked as Craig led them to the great room. "He's just making some calls to his work in the bedroom."

"Yes, please," Maggie answered.

Morgan indicated Maggie should take a seat. She sat in one of two cream upholstered chairs that faced a matching sectional. Miranda disappeared down a hall to the right.

"I'll get Kate," Morgan said. "She's with Ellie in the back yard."

"Thank you," Maggie said.

She watched him as he opened the sliding door and walked around the corner of the pool and out of sight. She looked around the room. A bouncy seat with a Noah's Ark theme sat on one corner of the huge blue rug. On the dining room table, several small piles of papers and pads were spread out and left, as though Morgan had been interrupted in the middle of something. Everything was neat and orderly and pretty, but Maggie could almost feel a Kristen-shaped hole in the house.

Miranda and her husband came into the room. Paul Cookson was more casually dressed in a pair of cargo shorts and a yellow polo shirt. Before they could speak, Morgan opened the sliding glass door and followed Kate into the house. She was holding Ellie. The little girl was dressed in a short romper in honor of the fine weather.

"Hello," Kate said as she came toward the living area.

"Good morning, Mrs. Newell," Maggie said. "Mr. Cookson."

Maggie waited as Kate settled Ellie into her bouncy seat and turned it on. Maggie could hear the vibration from across the room. Paul sat down on one side of the sectional with his wife, and Kate sat next to Morgan on the other.

"How are all of you doing?" Maggie asked.

Morgan nodded. "We're okay," he said, without any real conviction.

"We're still…. trying to accept things," Kate said. Maggie noticed the swelling below her eyes.

"I understand," Maggie said kindly. "Everyone has to deal with something like this in their own way, and everyone has their own timetable. Try not to feel like you have to be okay."

Morgan and Kate both nodded, though Kate was watching Ellie.

"I'm sorry to come by unannounced," Maggie said. "I just have a few things to talk to you about." She folded her hands on her knees, tried to look accessible and non-threatening. "We've narrowed down the time at which Kristen drowned. It was somewhere between 8pm and midnight Wednesday."

"Oh!" Kate cried out. "I was on my way! To help find her. I was coming!"

Morgan held out a tissue box from the coffee table, but Kate shook her head and took a deep breath.

Maggie gave her a moment before she went on. "The medical examiner has also determined that someone intentionally drowned Kristen. She didn't commit suicide."

The room was nearly silent for a moment, the only sound the vibration of the baby seat. Maggie looked around at Kristen's family. Craig Morgan sat with his mouth open just slightly, staring at the coffee table in front of him. Kate covered her face with her hands, but she didn't cry. Miranda and Paul shook their heads, almost in unison.

"That doesn't make any sense," Craig said quietly after a moment. "She's a stay-at-home mom." He looked at Maggie. "I mean, she doesn't really even know anybody here."

"It's possible that this started out as a carjacking, and just went very wrong," Maggie said, comfortable with the murky truth of it. "Or, Kristen might have been taken for other reasons."

"What other reasons?"

"We don't know that yet, Mr. Morgan, but I promise you that we're doing our best to find out." Maggie pulled out her small notebook and pen. "One of the most important things in cases like this one is to not waste time investigating people who had nothing to do with it. I need to find out where each of you was between eight and midnight Wednesday."

"You think someone here would hurt my wife?" Morgan cried.

"Actually, in spite of the fact that most victims are murdered by a spouse or family member, we have no reason to think any one of you did anything wrong," Maggie replied calmly. "But we do have to account for your whereabouts that night."

"I understand," he said more quietly. "Just please understand that this is...this is just foreign to us, being in this kind of situation."

"I do understand that," Maggie said kindly. "And I don't want to add unnecessary anxiety to your pain. Like I said, none of you is under suspicion. We just have to follow protocol for this kind of case."

"I didn't get here until Friday afternoon," Paul volunteered quietly. "I got here a couple of hours before you came to tell us about Kristen."

Maggie nodded. "What time did you leave Jacksonville, Mr. Cookson?"

"We had a general manager's meeting until 11am, and I left immediately after."

Maggie took notes. "Is there someone we can call to verify that?"

"Uh, Norman Best, the regional director. 904-672-7891."

Maggie wrote that down. "Thank you." She looked at Miranda.

"I was here, with Ellie," she said. "Craig had to pick Kate up in Tallahassee. I mean, I don't have anybody to—it was just Ellie and I."

"Don't worry about that," Maggie said reassuringly. She looked at Kate, who was staring at her hands in her lap. "What time did your flight get in, ma'am?"

Kate swallowed, and seemed to make an effort to rouse herself. "Well, I was late," she said, her voice husky. "The connection from Atlanta, I mean. I was supposed to get in at 8:15, but we didn't land until nine."

"What airline was that?"

"Oh." Kate blinked her eyes a few times. "Southwest. That's right."

"Okay, thank you. What time did you leave here for Tallahassee?" she asked Craig.

"I left around quarter after six," he answered. "I didn't know the flight was delayed until I got to the airport around eight."

"Okay. And when did the two of you get back here?"

He looked at Kate questioningly, but her eyes were focused on her lap. He looked back at Maggie. "It was about eleven."

"It was right after eleven," Miranda offered. "The news had just come on."

"That's right, we were watching the news when they got back," Paul said.

"Okay," Maggie said, taking notes. She looked up. "And were you all here the rest of the night? Did anybody go out?"

Kate didn't respond. The others shook their heads.

"There was no reason to go anywhere," Craig answered. "We talked for a couple of hours, about Kristen, about what was being done, and then we all went to bed."

"Around one or one-thirty, I think," Miranda said. "I gave Ellie her 12:30 bottle first."

"Okay, thank you," Maggie said. She closed her notepad. "Do you have any questions for me?"

Morgan looked over at Kate and swallowed before he looked back at Maggie. "How do...how do you know someone did this to her?"

Maggie wanted to share as little of that as possible, but she'd been prepared to answer. "There's some physical evidence to suggest she was held down," Maggie said.

At that, Kate began to quietly cry.

"I'm sorry, Mrs. Newell," Maggie said.

Morgan opened his mouth to say something, then looked at Kate and seemed to check himself.

"Did you have a question, Mr. Morgan?" Maggie asked.

"No," he answered quietly.

"I sent you an email with a waiver attached, allowing me to talk to Kristen's therapist."

"I'm sorry, I haven't been on the computer today."

"That's fine. If you could sign it and send it to her doctor, I'd appreciate it. What's her doctor's name and phone number?"

"Genna Drummond," he answered. He pulled his phone out of his back pocket and started tapping. "I don't know if she works Saturdays, but her number is 513-928-4453."

Maggie jotted it down and stood up. "I need to get back to the office," she said. "I'm very sorry to have brought you this news, but I promise that we'll be working very hard for Kristen."

Morgan stood. "I'll walk you out."

Maggie headed for the hallway, with Morgan right behind. He opened the door for her, followed Maggie out onto the little porch, and pushed the door almost closed.

"Lt. Redmond," he started. Maggie stopped and turned. "Did...do you know if Kristen suffered?"

"It would have been quick," Maggie answered. It wasn't true and didn't really answer his question.

He nodded slowly. "Thank you."

"You have my card," Maggie said. "Please call me if you need anything."

Maggie spent most of the day going over the background checks on the Morgans and the Cooksons. They didn't bother with Kate. There was no question about her being in Ohio until after Kristen was killed. There was also no question, for Maggie, that the woman was devastated.

Craig Morgan had no criminal record. He had a number of speeding tickets in his past, all paid, but seemed to have reformed once moving to FL. Or maybe since he'd had a child.

He had a BA in Business from Ohio State, and the Subaru in the garage was registered in his name. As background checks went, his was pretty uninteresting thus far.

His sister was only slightly more interesting. In 2000, she'd been arrested for simple assault. She'd pled no contest and received six months' probation. When Maggie called Cincinnati PD and had them look it up, it turned out to be a physical altercation over a man. The other one, a girl really, had also pled out and received the same sentence. Maggie did the math. Miranda Cookson, Morgan at the time, had only been twenty-two, and she hadn't been in trouble since.

She'd married Paul Cookson in 2003. Fifteen years and no children. Maggie wondered if that was intentional, or if they were unable to have a child.

Paul Cookson also had a smear on his record, though a minor one. He'd been involved in a road rage incident in 2014. Apparently, it was mutual; and over a fender bender at a red light. The other guy had thrown a shoe at Cookson's car, Cookson had pushed him to the ground. It went down as misdemeanor disturbing the peace, with the night each spent in jail considered time served.

Maggie had left a message with Dr. Drummond's answering service and stressed that it was a police matter and urgent. She'd gotten off the phone with her when Wyatt showed up in her doorway, tapping a file against his leg.

"Hey," he said.

"Hey."

"You want to go over Morgan's financials?"

"Yeah," Maggie answered.

Wyatt walked across the small room to Terry Coyle's desk, and wheeled his desk chair over to the other side of Maggie's desk.

"This has got to be more comfortable," he said.

"Terry's out with sciatica," Maggie mentioned.

"I won't sit long," Wyatt said, as he sat down. "Okay, so all of those financial details that tend to go to motive are missing."

"How so?"

Wyatt pulled his reading glasses out of his pocket and slipped them on. "Dwight's working on Morgan's business. I've been going after the personal stuff."

"Okay."

"Life insurance," he said, reading the file. "Morgan took out policies on himself and his wife right after they got married, but it was 500k on him and only two-fifty on her. A few weeks after their daughter was born, Morgan raised his payout to one-mil but Kristen's stayed the same."

Two-fifty is still a lot of money," Maggie said.

"Yeah, but it's not the smoking gun we like to see. What is that you're drinking?"

Maggie looked at her plastic cup from the gas station." Sweet tea," she answered.

"Never mind." Wyatt looked back down at the file in his lap. "They have a crap-ton of debt. They went for the lowest down payment possible on the house and they have a $420,000 mortgage. Both cars are financed, and Kristen's loan is new. According to his tax returns, Morgan's income's increased pretty markedly in the last three years. In other words, they've got a lot more debt than they should be comfortable with, but the bills are getting paid."

"That's inconvenient," Maggie said.

"It is," Wyatt agreed. "I haven't met the guy. What's your take on him?"

Maggie shrugged. "Based on experience, I know he's our best candidate. But I don't get the guilty vibe from him." She tapped her pen against her desk. "Most guilty people get defensive pretty quickly. He's been more concerned with defending his wife."

Wyatt nodded, then looked at the doorway as Dwight walked through it.

"Hey, y'all," he said.

"Hey, Dwight," Maggie said. "What's up?"

"Well, that guy Mike finally called me back. Kristen's college friend? He's been on a cruise with his wife. Mexico."

"Okay," Maggie said.

"Anyhow, he got real upset when I told him Kristen was dead. Actually, he told me he'd call me back in a few minutes, then he hung up. But he called back about ten minutes later. I didn't tell him somebody killed her. I figure the family can do that."

"So, what did he have to say?" Wyatt asked.

"Well, he said as far as he knew, Kristen was pretty happy lately. I reckon he was her best friend, cause last time he talked to her—" he looked down at his notes.

"She called him to tell him bon voyage and whatnot— last Friday. A week ago, yesterday, I mean."

"Okay."

"Anyhow, last time they talked, she told him she was doing really good, and that she was off her medication. Thing is, she said her doctor took her off. He thought that didn't sound like a good idea, but he let it go."

"Did he say how she sounded that last time?" Maggie.

"Just that she was really tired. Ellie's teething."

Maggie nodded. "Maybe she was tired, maybe she was feeling the effects of not taking her medication."

"Yeah," Dwight answered. "One other thing. When I asked him about how their marriage was going and whatnot, he mentioned that when Kristen told him she and Morgan were getting married, she mentioned that he broke his engagement to another girl the year before they met. Cause he didn't think he wanted to settle down and have kids yet. She felt kinda good about that, like he was sure this time."

"So how did he say the marriage was?"

Dwight shrugged. "He said it seemed to be going good. I mean, he said they didn't have a lot of time together 'cause Craig was working all the time, but he said Craig seemed like he loved her."

"What about her?" Maggie asked.

"Oh, she was definitely in love," Dwight answered.

"Okay. How's the other stuff going?"

"Well, pretty good," he answered, flipping a page in his notes. "Craig Morgan started his business back in Cincinnati, like they said. But it was just rental properties he inherited. He didn't actually incorporate until 2011, when he started buying more places and flippin' them and such. Then he sold the rentals." Dwight looked up at them. "Real good profit, too, since his mom had 'em all paid off. Then looks like he took all that money and started flippin' commercial properties, too. He's doin' some owner financing now, too."

"Is he still doing the same thing here, or does he just have the Ohio stuff?" Maggie asked.

"No, he's got like six or seven places here," Dwight answered. "Right now, I mean. He bought and flipped two already. One's up for sale, one's under contract, and he's done owner financing on the rest."

"Good money?" Maggie asked.

"I reckon," Dwight said. "More than I'm making, that's for sure. Probably more than all three of us together." He read his notes. "He's buying the places cheap and selling 'em for a good penny more than his mortgage payments. He's got three in Eastpoint, one in St. Joe, two in Carrabelle and he's the one bought that little place down the block from The Pig. That chiropractor's got a loan with him."

"Okay." Maggie got up and stretched her back.

"Oh, somethin' else that's maybe interesting," Dwight said. "Morgan ran for County Commissioner back in

Cincinnati. Seven years ago. He lost. But that lady I talked to from First Baptist down here, she said they told her he was planning to run down here, eventually. Not sure what for."

"Huh," Maggie said.

"Huh," Wyatt agreed.

"Reckon it's cool for me to head on home?" Dwight asked. He was supposed to have been off.

"Yeah, go ahead," Maggie answered, looking at her watch. "It's after three."

"Alrighty, then," Dwight said. "See y'all later."

Wyatt and Maggie watched him go, then Maggie looked at Wyatt. "I'm gonna hang around for a little while, wait for her doctor to call me back. Are you done with that?" she asked, nodding at his file.

"This is your copy," he answered, handing it to her. "I'm heading home. Don't forget we have dinner at your parents' tonight."

"I won't," Maggie said, already reading. "Six o'clock."

"You may kiss me," he said, leaning over her desk.

"Oh, thank you," she said. She gave him a quick kiss. "I was wondering if you'd given it up."

"You're a delight," he said as he headed for the door. "I was actually thinking we should do some heavy making out in their driveway. Your dad always finds that entertaining."

Maggie put both front windows down as she got onto the bridge, headed back to Apalach. The air was only a little cool, and Maggie breathed of it deeply, letting the salt and damp soothe her.

She'd finally gotten to talk to Dr. Drummond. Apparently, for the last two years, Kristen's therapy sessions had been monthly, first in Cincinnati, and then via phone when Kristen moved to Florida. But she had postponed the last appointment. Dr. Drummond had urged Kristen to find a local therapist, but she had dragged her heels. Dr. Drummond continued to write her prescriptions, phoned into the CVS in Apalach. She had not, by any means, agreed to or suggested that Kristen stop taking the medications. When Maggie had faxed the medical information waiver to CVS and asked, the pharmacist said that her meds were last refilled two weeks ago. Kristen had never picked them up.

Maggie's brain was weary from sorting facts, and from thinking about Kristen. Thinking about Kristen trying to spit out sand without swallowing water. Wondering if her last thought had been that she would miss Ellie so much. Wondering if she'd be able to get both of them some justice. She forced herself to shut it off, to focus on the air and the wind and the scents of the bay.

Ten minutes later, Maggie dropped the mail on the dining room table, kicked off her shoes, and gave Coco one last rub before heading into the kitchen. Stoopid beat her to the refrigerator, and began his quiet little pleas for it to dump out its contents. She gave him a piece of lettuce, grabbed an RC for herself, and went around the corner to the hall. "I'm home," she called out. "Sky, you have something from the financial aid department."

Kyle popped his head out his doorway. "Hi, Mom."

"Hey, buddy. Have you had your shower yet? We have to be at Grandma and Granddad's in like twenty minutes."

"Yeah, I took it after lunch."

"Okay," Maggie answered, as Sky came out of her room and headed her way.

"Hey," Sky said.

"Hey. You have some mail."

"Okay," Sky walked past Maggie and went to the table.

"How's your day been?" Maggie asked.

"Okay, I guess," Sky answered as she found her mail. "I've been going through my clothes, getting rid of stuff."

She opened the envelope with her thumb. "I seriously could not fit a run-over cat in that closet."

"That's a great image," Maggie said.

"Yeah," Sky answered distractedly as she read.

A moment later, eyes wide, she looked up at Maggie. "Mom," she said in a hush.

"What's wrong?"

"I got a full ride," Sky answered.

Maggie headed over to the table, her heart rate speeding up just a bit.

"I mean, tuition, books, on-campus housing," Sky said. "I mean, that's everything, right?"

Maggie stopped beside her daughter. "I thought you already heard from everything you applied for."

"Yeah, me, too," Sky answered. "But they were all like a thousand here, five-hundred there."

"Maybe your financial aid counselor put you in for something else," Maggie said. "Where's it from?"

Sky read for a moment, moving to the second page. "Oh, crap," she said, barely above a whisper. She looked up at Maggie. "Crap, Mom."

"What?"

"It's the Grace Cunningham Memorial Fund."

Maggie's chest constricted. "What?"

Sky handed her the letter, pointing to the middle of the second page. There it was; the Grace Cunningham Memorial Fund.

Maggie saw Grace running toward her across a grungy yard, saw her kissing her baby's cheek. Saw her pale, skinny arms as her body was hauled onto the Coast Guard cutter.

"I don't understand," Maggie said quietly.

And then she did.

⚓ ⚓ ⚓

Maggie's parents lived on one of the few residential properties on the bay side of Hwy 98, just outside of Apalach. As Maggie turned left onto the long, gravel driveway, she saw that Wyatt was just getting out of his truck. A few minutes later, Gray let them into the house.

They followed him into the big, bright, eat-in-kitchen that looked out onto the back deck, the expansive yard, and the dock that meandered out onto the water.

"Hey, y'all," Georgia Redmond said from the stove.

Everyone said their 'hellos' and Wyatt walked over to stand behind Georgia, where he loomed over her shoulder. "That smells amazing."

"Beef stew with dumplings," Georgia said, as she accepted his kiss on the cheek. "And some lemon pie for dessert."

Gray, almost as tall as Wyatt and too skinny for his height, pushed back a lank of gray hair that had fallen over his brow. "We also ordered a couple of pizzas for you, Wyatt, in case you're still hungry."

"Witty," Wyatt said, as Georgia gave him a wooden spoon to lick. "I'm wondering if I should be marrying your wife."

"Hey," Maggie said.

"That would be inefficient, Wyatt," Gray said smoothly. "You marry the daughter, you get the wife for free."

"Y'all quit flirting till after we've had dinner," Georgia said. She looked over at Sky and Kyle, who had settled at the long farmhouse table her father had built from old barn wood. "Can you kids set the table for us?"

The kids got up and started grabbing what they needed from the cabinets. Wyatt walked over to Maggie, stood behind her, and draped an arm around her neck.

"You fancy losing a game of Scrabble later, Wyatt?" Gray asked.

Wyatt opened his mouth to answer but Maggie flicked at him over her shoulder.

"Shut up, I'm starving," she said.

⚓   ⚓   ⚓

The sun had set by the time dinner had been eaten and the kids started cleaning up. Gray and Wyatt were enjoying a couple of beers while the women nursed their sweet teas.

They'd watched the reflection on the bay change from yellow to orange and then, for just a moment, to red, before dark joined dark and there wasn't much difference between water and sky.

Everyone celebrated with Sky when she shared her news. When Georgia had asked about the scholarship, Sky had told her about the Grace Cunningham Memorial

Fund. Georgia had just proclaimed it wonderful. Wyatt had caught Maggie's eye when she'd said it, though, and she knew he knew where the scholarship had come from. When she'd looked over at Gray, he was staring at her, and she'd guessed that all three of them knew its provenance. She'd been grateful that it hadn't been discussed.

"Y'all," Gray said now, as he slowly turned his beer bottle round and round. "Georgia and I have something we want to discuss with you," he said. He looked over at the kids, who were just closing the dishwasher. "Kids, you, too. Y'all come over here."

Maggie felt something closing up in her throat. "What's wrong, Daddy?"

Gray had had lung cancer just a couple of years ago, and the loss of him was one of her most potent fears.

"Calm yourself, Sunshine, it's nothing bad."

"It's not," Georgia said quickly.

Maggie looked quickly at her mother to check her face. Her mother had never seemed to have much of a poker face, and was inclined to lie. The truth that her perfect mother had cheated on her perfect father once had blind-sided Maggie. That the act led to her biological father being a man she had no business associating with, but had come to call her friend, was even more devastating.

Over the last few months, Maggie had gradually tried to close the distance that she had between herself and her mom. They had never discussed the issue, not once, and maybe they didn't need to.

Now, she looked at Georgia's face, so strikingly pretty, and saw no artifice.

"What's up, Granddad?" Sky asked, as the kids sat back down.

Gray looked down the table at his wife, then looked at Maggie and Wyatt. "We have an idea, and we want y'all to hear us out, because I sense some argument afoot."

The rest of them nodded or said okay. Gray sat up a bit straighter before he went on.

"It's about your housing situation."

"What housing situation?" asked Maggie.

"The one you're in," her dad replied. He held up a hand. "Hear me out a minute. What Georgia and I propose is that, after the wedding, y'all come live here."

That wasn't any of the things Maggie expected him to say. She shook her head. "What? All of us?"

"No, Sunshine. Just you four."

"What's going on?" Wyatt asked.

"What Gray's trying to say is we're suggesting we trade houses," Georgia said, smiling.

"What?" Maggie looked at her father. "Why?"

"For a number of very good reasons," he answered. "And I want you to listen to them before you start getting up in arms. First of all, Wyatt's a good man, and he's fine with moving out there to Bluff Road, but that's got to be a hard thing, and y'all know it."

Wyatt held up a hand. "I appreciate what you're saying, Gray, I really do. But, honestly, it'll take me a little bit to feel at home, but I'm fine with it."

"Wyatt, marriage is challenging enough, especially with a treat like Maggie here. Starting your married life in a house that wasn't occupied by your wife's first husband gives you a much better chance of being happy."

"I'm happy," Wyatt said simply.

"You're *happy* about getting married. You're *willing* to be married there. Two different things."

"Seriously," Wyatt said. "They don't feel very different." He looked at Maggie. "I don't need you to move. If we decide down the road that we want to buy a place, we can." He looked at Gray, then Georgia. "That's what we've pretty much decided."

"You really want to take on a mortgage—an Apalach-sized mortgage—at your ages? It'll probably outlive you." Gray put his palms down on the table. "Besides, we have other reasons for wanting to do this. That place is too small for you, it always has been. But now that Maggie's grown up, *this* place is too *big* for us. Besides, I grew up in that house. I love it, and you know it, Maggie."

"What about Mom? Mom's a town girl—" she started.

"It was my idea," Georgia interrupted quietly.

Maggie looked at her. "Why? You're a town girl, Mom. And you have your garden, and you guys have been doing so much work on this place."

"I know that," Georgia said. "But your Daddy and I are in a new season of our lives. I've got him all to myself now, and we still have twenty, thirty years. We're both ready for change, for something different."

Maggie looked at her mother for a moment before she spoke. "Mom, do you have any other reason for doing this?" she asked carefully.

"I know what you're thinking, Maggie, and no."

There were several seconds of silence around the table.

"What? Mr. Boudreaux?" Sky asked. Everyone else at the table looked her way. "You guys, it's not like we all haven't talked about it."

That was true. A few months back, not wanting to keep the same secret her parents had kept from her, Maggie had told the kids about Boudreaux being her biological father. It had been something of a shock. They'd known *of* him their whole lives. He was too big a feature of the town for them not to. But the first time they'd really been around him was in the middle of a hurricane, when Boudreaux had saved all of their lives, and then they had saved his.

Despite the immediate shock, the kids had pretty much taken it in stride. As they said, this kind of thing happened all the time these days, and their Granddad was still their Granddad.

After another uncomfortable silence, Maggie looked at the kids, then back at her father. "What about the kids?"

she asked. "They love Wyatt, and they're excited about being a family, but their memories of their dad are there."

"Mom, Dad's everywhere," Sky said.

"Can I say something?" All eyes turned to Kyle. "Yeah, we have lots of memories there, but it's not like strangers would be moving into our house. I'm sure we'll hang out with Grandma and Granddad same as we always do. The memories will still be there."

Maggie looked at her son, the image of his father, a boy who had always seemed too old for his age.

"Is that what you think, buddy?" she asked him.

He shrugged. "Yeah, I'm cool with it. Serious."

Maggie sighed. She looked at her father. "What about the girls? What about Stoopid?"

"I was kinda hoping Stoopid goes with the house," Wyatt said.

"Stoopid goes with me," Maggie replied.

"Maggie," Gray said, holding up a hand. "It'd take Wyatt and I a weekend to build a coop and a new run out in the yard."

Maggie looked over at Sky.

"Mom, I'm perfectly cool with it," she said. "I'm leaving in August, and I'm looking at seven years of school. I have a room here already, anyway."

"That's a good point, too," Kyle said. "We already have rooms here."

"And you guys could take our room or the guest room," Georgia encouraged.

Maggie looked at Wyatt. "Wyatt?"

Wyatt sighed, and seemed to take a moment to choose his words. "Look, I'm fine either way, I really am. Probably finer with being here. Like I said, I'll probably feel at home here sooner than I will at your place. But I'm not asking you to give up your home. I won't do it, so you and the kids need to decide."

"But you're giving up your home," Maggie said quietly.

"My house is a rental. And I'm giving it up either way, right?"

"It's up to you, Mom," Sky said kindly. "We're cool with it."

Maggie stared at her tea a moment. She was overwhelmed with the need to do the right things for the people sitting at that table, the people that were her life.

"Tell you what, y'all," Wyatt said, standing. "Let's let this settle a little while. I have to use the facilities. Then we'll all try not to make fun of Wyatt while we play some Scrabble. Then you can give us your decision, Maggie."

Maggie huffed out an attempt at a laugh. "That long?"

"Your nuptials are imminent, Sunshine."

⚓ ⚓ ⚓

Almost two hours later, Maggie sat on the bottom step of the back deck. It had turned a little windy and cool, and the several palms in the yard sounded like they were whispering to each other. There was a slight chop on the bay, and the fenders of Gray's wooden oyster skiff bumped rhythmically against the dock.

Maggie heard the sliding glass door open and shut behind her. A moment later, Wyatt's feet appeared on either side of hers, and he sat down two steps above her. He wrapped his arms around her waist, put his chin on top of her head. They sat in silence for several moments before Maggie spoke.

"If I said I wanted to move here, would you be happy?"

"No happier than I am already, but I would like it here, sure. And I think your folks are telling the truth. I don't think they're just trying to do something kind."

"And if I said I wanted to stay in my house?"

"Then we'd do that. And we'd be fine."

Maggie thought about Wyatt in her room, trying not to feel like he was sitting on another man's bed.

"I want to tell them we'll trade houses."

Wyatt kissed her temple, then let out a breath. "Then that's what we'll do. I would like to enter into negotiations about the rooster, though," he said lightly.

"Stoopid goes where I go," Maggie said, smiling.

"Then I go where Stoopid goes," Wyatt said.

"Scholarship, huh? Wyatt asked after a moment.

"Yeah."

"So, I imagine you'll be talking to Boudreaux soon."

"I imagine so."

TWELVE

ennett Boudreaux sat at the round, antique maple table in his kitchen. Light streamed in through the large window beside it, making his lightly-graying brown hair look almost blond. He poured himself a second cup of chicory coffee and added a bit of cream.

Amelia, his tall, Creole housekeeper and cook, stood at the island stove, presiding over one slice of sizzling bacon.

Boudreaux had just taken a sip of his coffee when a dog began barking outside. He put down his cup, and he and Amelia both listened. He wasn't sure, but it sounded like the dog was in his yard.

"Hell you say!" came the faint sound of Miss Evangeline yelling outside.

"Damn it," Boudreaux muttered.

"You need to get up out that chair and go get Mama," Amelia snapped at him, despite the fact that he was already rising.

The dog continued to bark, though it didn't exactly sound menacing. As Boudreaux stepped out onto the back porch, the barking was halted by a sharp whine, and Boudreaux saw the neighbor's German Shephard running back toward his own yard.

Miss Evangeline, standing on the brick path between her cottage and the main house, was flinging her aluminum walker after him. It landed about three feet away.

"Come on, puppy!" Miss Evangeline yelled. "I pass you another slap!"

Boudreaux started down the porch steps. "What the hell are you doing?" he snapped.

"Puppy come over here Mr. Benny yard and take one my tenny ball! Yank it right off, he do!"

Boudreaux stopped and picked up her walker. As she'd said, one of the two green tennis balls was missing.

"You can't just go around slapping German Shepherds," he said, roughly setting the walker down in front of her.

Miss Evangeline's red-checked house dress billowed in the breeze, and she tugged her blue bandana down over her ears. Her light brown skin, wearing a hundred years' worth of wrinkles, seemed almost yellow in the morning sun. "Ain't the puppy yard," she said, craning her neck to look up at him. "Ain't his tenny ball, neither, no."

Boudreaux sighed and started back toward the porch steps. "There's a reason Hitler had Shepherds, you know."

Miss Evangeline made a clicking sound behind him. "Call him up tell him he come get this one, too! I don't tolerate it, no!"

Boudreaux sighed as he opened the kitchen door.

Miss Evangeline settled down a bit once she'd sat down at the table and been served her breakfast. Boudreaux was taking a sip of his lukewarm coffee when the front door bell rang.

Amelia put her cast iron pan on the drainboard and started out of the room.

"It's probably the neighbor, wanting me to pay for a therapist for his dog," Boudreaux said.

But when Amelia came back into the kitchen, it was Maggie who followed her. Boudreaux smiled. Miss Evangeline chewed her toast.

"Maggie," Boudreaux said, standing. "This is a pleasant surprise."

"I'm sorry, I didn't mean to interrupt your breakfast," Maggie replied.

"Forget it," Boudreaux said.

"Today ice cream day," Miss Evangeline stated, glaring up at Maggie through her thick glasses. "We go the ice cream."

"Today is ice cream day," Maggie said to her. "But later on. I have some work to do first."

"Would you like some coffee?" Boudreaux asked.

"No. Thank you, but I just have a minute."

He pulled a chair out. "Would you like to sit down?"

"Actually, could we talk privately?"

He hesitated just for a second. "Of course. Let's go out on the porch."

Maggie followed him out, smiling at Miss Evangeline as she passed. Boudreaux held the door for her, then closed it behind him. They walked across the wraparound porch, and settled into two white Adirondack chairs.

"How are you?" Boudreaux asked, his sharp blue eyes curious.

"I'm fine, thank you," Maggie answered. "How are you?"

Boudreaux nodded. He waited for her to speak.

"The Grace Cunningham Memorial Fund," Maggie said.

Boudreaux nodded again.

"You," she stated simply.

Boudreaux rested his chin on his fist. "You told me once that with my money and influence, I was in a position to help girls like Grace."

"I did."

"If it makes you feel any more comfortable, there are three other young women from Franklin County who received the same scholarship. There will be four more next year."

"And one of them will be Sky?" Maggie asked.

"If she maintains a 3.5, yes," he replied. "You disapprove."

Maggie shrugged. "I can't say that I disapprove. She is your granddaughter. But why not just offer your help straight out? Why make up a scholarship?"

"Create, not make up," Boudreaux said. "I did it partly because she's my grandchild, and partly for Grace. But, also because the last time I tried to send a girl through law school, she turned it down."

Maggie stared at him a moment. "Me?"

"Yes."

"When?"

"When you were accepted," he answered. "I offered to give the money to your parents. But when they got back to me, they said that you refused it."

It took Maggie a moment to answer. "They said they had enough savings. I didn't believe them," she said. "I thought they were going to take out a second mortgage."

"I'm sorry," he said. "If we'd told you the truth sooner, you might have gone."

Maggie sighed and looked out at the yard. His dozen or so mango trees, unusual this far north, were beginning to set fruit. She'd been so devastated when she'd had to give up her plans to become a prosecutor. She'd busted her butt to get into FSU's law school, but she'd come home and become a cop, like her grandfather.

"It's okay," she said finally. "It worked out the way it was supposed to." She looked back over at Boudreaux. "And you are her grandfather, even if you don't really know each other."

The kids had met him a few months back, and they'd all had lunch together once. But, they were all still tip-toeing a bit.

"I saw Sky the other day," he said. "Going into that dress shop on Commerce."

Maggie nodded. "She was looking for a dress for the wedding."

They stared at each other for a moment, the silence comfortable.

"Are you sure you won't come?" she asked.

"I'm sure," Boudreaux said. "It wouldn't be very fair to your parents. In their home, no less."

"They said they were okay with it."

"Of course, they did," he said gently.

Maggie sighed. "I suppose." She stood up, and he quickly stood as well. "I really do have to get to work. Tell Miss Evangeline I'll be back around one."

"I will," he said, his incredible eyes focusing on hers.

Maggie faltered for a moment, took a step forward, then stopped. Then she stepped up to him and clumsily put her arms around his neck. He gently wrapped his arms around her.

"It's always good to see you, Maggie," he said into her hair.

⚓ ⚓ ⚓

Maggie was halfway across the bridge to Eastpoint when her phone rang from its holder on her dash. She glanced at the number, then connected the call and put it on speaker.

"This is Maggie," she answered.

"Lt. Redmond?" The voice was husky, a woman of middle age or with a bad smoking habit.

"Yes."

"This is Donna Lindquist, with Corrections. I'm a guard."

"Hello," Maggie said.

"I saw the report about that woman that drowned out at Lake Morality."

"Okay."

"Well, it might be nothing, but it said y'all were looking for anyone that might have seen something Wednesday night."

Maggie sat up a little bit straighter and slowed her speed. "Yes, we are."

"Well, I work second shift, three to eleven," Donna said. "When I was driving home on Lake Morality Road, right when I was passing the turn-off there, I saw a truck getting ready to pull out from the access road."

"What kind of truck?"

"I'm not sure. I don't really know trucks," she said. "I couldn't see the front, just the side of the front, you know what I mean?"

"Yeah."

"It wasn't one of those little jobs, though. It was a big one. Not as big as my husband's Ram, though, I don't think."

"What color was it?"

"Well, it was dark, and I didn't slow down or anything. I mean, people go out there at night all the time," she answered. "There's no lights on that road, so it was pretty dark, but seemed like it was black, or a really dark blue."

"Did you notice anything else about the truck? A tool box, antenna topper, anything?"

"No, I'm sorry," Donna said. "But the paint was shiny. I'd say it wasn't any older than five or six years. I don't feel like I thought it was new when I was looking at it. But definitely taken care of."

"Okay," Maggie said. "Did you see them pull out behind you while you were going down the road? Or did you see them pull onto 98 at all?"

"I glanced in the rear view when I was getting onto 98," the woman answered. "They weren't behind me then. If they pulled out later, I didn't notice. I pulled out ahead of a Texaco truck."

"Okay," Maggie said. "I really appreciate you calling."

"I should have turned around and taken a look," the woman said. Maggie heard sadness in her voice.

"Listen, Donna. Whoever was in the truck might be a witness, not a suspect," Maggie said. "Or maybe they got there before or after this happened. She might have already been at the bottom of the lake."

The other woman was silent for a moment. "Well," she said finally. "I can't help that I'm gonna think about that for a while. You know what I mean?"

Maggie sighed quietly. "Yes, I do."

When Maggie walked into the SO, Louanne held a finger up to get her attention.

"Hey, Maggie, I saw you pull up," she said. "Kate Newell's on line seven."

"Okay, thank you," Maggie said without slowing. She waved at Dwight as she went past his office, then dumped her purse on her desk and picked up the phone.

"Hello, Mrs. Newell, this is Maggie Redmond," she said.

"Hello," the other woman said. "I don't mean to bother you, but I was wondering if you've learned anything new yet."

"No, ma'am," Maggie answered. "We are working on a few things, and I will call you when I have something worth reporting."

"Thank you," Kate said, clearly disappointed.

"Mrs. Newell, I understand how badly you need answers right now," Maggie said. "I promise that we're working very hard to get those for you."

She heard Kate Newell sigh softly. "I understand, Lieutenant. I'm very grateful for all of your help."

Kate hung up, and Maggie rubbed at her face to clear her mind. Then she walked back down the hall. Dwight was still at his desk.

"Hey, Maggie," he said.

"Hey. We might have something good," she said. "One of the guards out at Correctional says she saw a truck coming out of Lake Morality Wednesday night."

Dwight grabbed a pen and a sticky pad.

"No plate. She barely saw it," Maggie said. "Dark blue or black truck, 3/4 ton or bigger, not a Ram. Actually, include Rams just in case. Late model."

Wyatt came up behind her. "You might want to add dark gray just in case, too. Memory's a trickster."

"Yeah, do that, Dwight," Maggie said.

"How wide you want it to go?" Dwight asked.

"There's gonna be a million of them around here," she answered. She looked at Wyatt. "What do you think? Start with just Franklin County?"

He nodded, frowning. "Yeah. Then if that doesn't pan out, we can try Wakulla. If he was willing to go as far as Carrabelle, he might live on the other side of it."

"Yeah," Maggie said. "Dwight, ask Mike to sort them by males with records first, then males without, then everybody else, ok?"

"Gotcha," he said, and picked up his desk phone.

Maggie walked back to her office, Wyatt behind her.

"How many of those things do you think we're gonna get?"

"Way too many," he answered. "But, I think you triaged it correctly."

"Maybe we can get some help from Apalach PD running them down," she said.

"Possibly. Let's see what Mike comes back with, how many of these trucks we're going to have to check," Wyatt said. "Then we can talk to Bledsoe about getting one or two other guys to help us out."

⚓ ⚓ ⚓

Three hours later, Wyatt and Maggie had paired up to check out the names from Eastpoint and Apalach. Dwight and Burt were working on addresses east of Eastpoint to the county line. Maggie and Wyatt had finished with the three Eastpoint trucks.

The strategy had been to say they were looking for someone who might have witnessed something that would help them with a case. When the truck owners said they hadn't, they'd been asked for their whereabouts between eight and midnight Wednesday, and those alibis had been verified via phone while they were still with the subject. It was an imperfect plan, as most were. If they were talking to their guy, he could have arranged his alibi ahead of time, and would bolt the minute they left. But it was what they had to work with.

In one case, the guy was in the ER for slicing his hand open on a piece of sheet metal. In another, the guy had been in custody at Apalach PD for pulling around to the drive through window at Burger King with no clothes on. Those were easy to scratch from the list.

Having eliminated the Eastpoint truck owners, Maggie and Wyatt decided to move on to checking out the Apalach prospects.

"You want to grab a quick bite at Papa Joe's before we start on these?" Wyatt asked, as they walked down the driveway of the last subject's house.

"Uh," Maggie looked at her watch. "How about a sandwich at Apalachicola Coffee?"

"Why? It's not 2:45."

They stopped at Maggie's Jeep, and Wyatt opened her door.

"Today's ice cream day," Maggie said.

"Ah, is it time to take Boudreaux's nanny out for a spin?"

"It is, yes," Maggie said, smiling. "I can get her some gelato, I get my coffee, and you can have a sandwich. Everybody's happy and we're in and out in half an hour."

FOURTEEN

Wyatt held the door as Miss Evangeline, followed by Maggie, toddled her way into Apalachicola Coffee. There were quite a few people there at one in the afternoon, and Maggie saw Kirk at the big sexy machine, waiting on a young couple that had, between them, more tattoos than you'd find on the average cargo ship.

The gelato case was near the door, and Maggie led Miss Evangeline there.

"I don't see why we go here," Miss Evangeline said. "Why we don't go the ice cream place?"

"This ice cream's better," Maggie said. She looked over the top of the gelato case. Spaz was boxing chocolates for two older ladies at the chocolate counter. "I have to go order my coffee. Figure out what kind you want and that guy over there will get it for you."

Miss Evangeline leaned over her walker, just shy of putting her face on the glass. "Why they write so tiny?" she asked. "Can't read nothin', me."

"They have mango," Maggie said. Miss Evangeline was the reason Boudreaux went through the time and expense of growing mangoes in his back yard.

"I get the mango," Miss Evangeline said, straightening up.

"Okay, he'll be over in a minute. Let me go get my coffee."

Maggie walked over to the coffee counter. Wyatt was standing behind the tattooed couple, who were paying for their order.

Maggie and Wyatt moved to let them by, then stepped up to the counter. Kirk looked at the two of them with an expression that was somewhere between boredom and coma.

"It's not 2:45," he said.

"I'm just here to eat," Wyatt said. "She's the one that's here out of turn."

"What can I get ya?" Kirk asked him.

"What's that pig sandwich you make?"

"The Hog," Kirk replied dryly.

"Pig, hog. I want that," Wyatt said.

"Okay." He looked at Maggie. She stared back for a moment.

"What?" Maggie asked him.

"Are you having a sandwich?"

"No, just coffee," she said.

"It's not ready."

Maggie jerked her thumb over her shoulder. "They just got coffee."

"Your coffee's not ready," he said. "I don't keep the Hurricane out here."

"Why not?

"Because you and I are the only ones that can drink it," he said. "It's gonna be a minute."

"Okay," Maggie said. "And I have a friend over there that needs some ice cream."

"We make gelato," Kirk said.

"I realize that. But don't tell her that. Just tell her it's ice cream."

"They're two different things," he said with an accompanying eyeroll.

"Not to her," Maggie snapped.

"Do you guys need some alone time?" Wyatt asked cheerfully.

Kirk sighed. "I'll go order your sandwich," he said, and walked around the corner to the kitchen.

"I think he's warming up to you," Wyatt said.

"I think I should start having somebody taste my coffee for me, like the kings used to do."

"Kinda pointless, since it would probably knock them out, poison or no poison."

Kirk came out of the kitchen, and Maggie saw him look over toward the gelato case.

"There's nobody over there," he said when he got back to the counter. "Why are you guys yanking my chain so hard today?"

Maggie turned around to look. She couldn't see Miss Evangeline, either. "She's over there," she said. "But she's little. You just have to look harder."

Kirk sighed. "Hey, Spaz! Gelato customer!" he called.

Spaz turned around slowly to look, then turned back again. "There's nobody there," he called back in a reedy voice.

"Where go the ice cream man?" Miss Evangeline barked from the void.

"That's her," Wyatt said.

$$\updownarrow \quad \updownarrow \quad \updownarrow$$

They decided to eat outside on one of the benches. Wyatt swallowed his sandwich whole while Maggie nursed her latte. Miss Evangeline sat between them, holding her cup of mango gelato right under her mouth as she ate. Maggie and Wyatt were discussing their case, unworried about Miss Evangeline; the only time she left the house was with Maggie.

"So, I'm thinking," Wyatt said, as he got up to throw his trash in a nearby can. "If none of these trucks pan out, we might want to add female owners to the list."

"Larry's report said it's unlikely that it's a woman," Maggie said. "He said we're looking for a men's size 11 at least. I have no idea what that would be in a woman's shoe."

"That's true," Wyatt said, sitting back down. "And even though it's most likely that the guy driving the truck is our killer, it's possible that the truck itself belongs to a woman. His wife or girlfriend or something."

"I see what you're saying," Maggie said.

"Less likely, but if we come up empty…" Wyatt said.

"Yeah," Maggie agreed. "But I don't see a woman having the strength to hold Kristen down with her foot until she drowned."

"Who drown?" Miss Evangeline asked.

"A woman," Maggie answered.

"Why somebody drowns her?"

"We don't know yet," Maggie answered.

"No, I don't think we're looking for a female killer, but we might be looking for her truck."

Wyatt watched Miss Evangeline as she scratched at the bottom of her cup with her plastic spoon. Once she'd just about scratched a hole in the cup, Wyatt held his hand out and she gave it to him.

"We need to get going," he said as he tossed it in the trash. "You ready to go, Miss Evangeline?"

"Law, yes," she said as Maggie got up and helped her stand. "I need go home, put some ointment on my asteroids."

Wyatt looked over at Maggie, who shrugged.

Miss Evangeline got her grip on her walker and peered up at Wyatt. "You watch, boy. You get an age, and alla sudden your ass on fire sundown to sundown."

Maggie watched Wyatt not make a remark.

"Well, okay then," Wyatt said, and leaned over behind the old lady to give Maggie a kiss. Miss Evangeline plopped her walker between them, just missing Wyatt's left foot.

"No time for that neither, no," she said. "Flames is lickin' at my underwears."

Wyatt smiled at the old lady's back as she maneuvered herself around the bench.

"Okey-doke," he said. He looked at Maggie. "Want to leave my truck here and go in yours?"

"Okay," Maggie said.

"I just need to run in and use the restroom."

He went back inside, and Maggie helped Miss Evangeline into the back seat of the car, then got in and started the engine. She rolled down the windows and then took some paperwork and a travel mug off the passenger seat, so Wyatt could sit.

"Mr. Benny mama drown, too," Miss Evangeline piped up from the back.

Maggie glanced at the old lady in her rear-view mirror. "I know. He told me."

"That your grandmama."

Maggie nodded.

"The bastard-man done it to her," Miss Evangeline stated. "Mr. Benny daddy."

Boudreaux had told Maggie the same thing once. He'd only been four or five at the time his mother had died.

"How do you know?"

"'Cause I see her," Miss Evangeline answered. "I see her head when they haul her out the bayou. They say she gone hit her head on a cypress stump or somethin' but I knew, and he don't care I know."

Maggie watched as the old lady pulled out her upper denture and looked at it, then put it back in her mouth.

"Juju got that one," Miss Evangeline said.

"He had a heart attack, right? After he moved here from Louisiana?"

"His heart don't kill him 'cause it feel like it," Miss Evangeline said. "I sent the juju after him, 'cause one day Mr. Benny gon' come here and cut his throat."

Maggie watched Wyatt come out of the coffee shop.

"Juju got him so Mr. Benny don't have to go the jail for killin' the bastard-man."

⚓   ⚓   ⚓

By six o'clock, Maggie and Wyatt had talked with all but two of the Apalach subjects. The first one, Bobby Trainer, was not at his house or his work, a body shop out on Bluff Road. His boss had said Trainer was off Mondays and Tuesdays. Trainer didn't sound very promising, really. He'd done two years at Franklin for felony possession, getting out on parole in 2016. A call to his parole officer yielded the information that Trainer had, thus far, been an outstanding parolee.

The other subject was a guy named William New-combe. He'd done four years in Tallahassee for armed robbery, getting out in 2004. He didn't have an employer or a parole officer that they knew of, and was nowhere to be found. A neighbor who was living in a marijuana cloud stated that he hadn't seen Newcombe in several days. Wyatt and Maggie were too tired and preoccupied to address the cloud.

"I think we should call it a day and try Trainer and Newcombe again in the morning, before we head over to the office," Wyatt said as they walked from the neighbor's sandy lot to the Jeep parked on the street. "What do you think?"

Maggie nodded. "That was Dwight that called while you were getting your secondhand high on the porch," she said. "They've talked to everyone on their list. Nothing. I told them to go on home."

Wyatt opened the Jeep door for Maggie and leaned on it. "Did you plan anything for dinner?"

"No. There's no school tomorrow, so Sky's going to the movies in Panama City with Bella. She dropped Kyle off at my folks', so he and Daddy can go out to the oyster beds in the morning."

"I'm never doing that again, by the way," Wyatt said.

"I know, you've told me."

"Five in the morning."

"I know," Maggie said.

"Okay, well, what do you feel like eating?"

"Do you feel like cooking?" Maggie asked.

"Not really."

"Me, neither," she said. "You want me to run out to Hong Kong Bistro and grab something?"

"I do," Wyatt answered. "Do you need to go home and take care of your herd first?"

Maggie shook her head. "No, the kids did."

"My house, then?"

"Sure," Maggie answered.

"Okey-doke, then I will go home and bathe."

"Goody. I like you when you've bathed," Maggie said as she got in the Jeep.

Wyatt shut her door. "And I like *you* when you're not speaking."

Maggie and Wyatt ate their dumplings and coconut shrimp at the bar that separated his kitchen from the dining area. A light rain had decided to fall. Wyatt had opened up the French doors that led from the dining area to the back patio, and they enjoyed the light breeze and the metallic, wet-dirt scent of the air.

"You ever make it over to the flower shop to order the bouquet?" Wyatt asked.

Maggie ate her last bite of shrimp. "No, I'm meeting Mom there in the morning."

"What time?"

"They don't open till 8:30."

"No biggie," Wyatt said. He picked up their paper plates and walked around the bar. "Come pick me up when you're done." He tossed their plates in the trash can.

"You want to go in the Jeep?" Maggie asked, as she handed him the empty take-out boxes.

"Yeah. Or my truck. Just no point in taking two vehicles."

"The Jeep's fine."

She watched as Wyatt opened the fridge. He always looked so huge in her tiny kitchen. His kitchen wasn't any bigger, but somehow, he seemed to fit better in it.

"You want to finish up that red wine?" he asked her.

"Sure."

He pulled the bottle out, then got two glasses out of a cabinet and started pouring.

"What?" he asked, but it was more statement than question.

"What what?"

He looked over at her. "Why are you looking at me like that?"

"Like what?" she asked, as he brought the wine over to the breakfast bar.

"Like you're about to tell me I have an inoperable toenail tumor," he answered. He stood on the other side of the bar and took a swig of his wine.

Maggie took a sip of hers and then shrugged.

"You look so at home here."

"I live here."

Maggie gave him a look and a sigh. "It's just that you're giving up so much."

"What are you saying?"

"That you've given up your job, a job that you loved and were amazing at, and now you're giving up your home."

Wyatt took another drink of his wine, then set it down on the tile. "So?"

"Wyatt."

"These are choices that I've made, Maggie," Wyatt said. "Choices."

"I know that," she said quietly. "But so much change. What if it doesn't make you happy?"

"Look," he said a little testily. "How long have we known each other?"

"Ten years."

"Eleven."

"Why did you ask me?"

"We've known each other for eleven years. Worked together every day," he said. "I was there when you got divorced, I was there when you killed your first human being, and I was there when David was killed. I've seen you at all of your worst times, and I've also been there for all of your good days, during which you're still an asspain. Don't you think that if you weren't what I needed, I would have figured that out already?"

Maggie swallowed and shrugged.

"We've been best friends for a long time, and I've been in love with you for six years," he said quietly.

"Two."

"It started ten minutes after you got divorced, and we've already agreed that you would have missed the whole damn thing if I hadn't finally told you."

"Don't snap at me," she snapped.

"I'm not snapping," he snapped back. "Look, you need to stop fretting over whether or not I know what I'm doing here. I'm about to embark on the most carefree existence known to man, because, for the rest of my life, you're gonna worry the crap out of everything before I get a chance to!"

Maggie sighed, and slowly turned her bar stool one way, and then the other.

"I just don't want you to regret it one day."

"I already do," he said quietly.

She looked over at him, and he smiled, his dimples deepening.

"Okay," she said. She gave him half a smile. "At least it won't be unexpected."

⚓ ⚓ ⚓

Maggie got out of the Jeep and crossed the street, met her mother on the sidewalk in front of the flower shop.

"Hi, Mom," Maggie said.

"Hey, sweetie."

Maggie gave her mother a kiss on the cheek. Georgia smelled like sunshine and good dirt, and her skin was warm and soft. Maggie missed hugging and kissing her mother, and she wondered when they'd be done walking on eggshells with each other. Most of the distance between them was Maggie's fault, and she knew it. She just wasn't sure how to get across it.

"Don't let me forget I need to get your daddy some propane when we're done," Georgia said. "He wants to grill some fish tonight."

"Sounds yummy," Maggie said as she opened the door for her mother.

"Do you want to come?" Georgia asked. "We have enough."

"I'm sorry, I can't," Maggie answered. "I really need to try to go to bed early tonight."

They stepped into the bright interior of the shop. The century-old ceilings were high and painted white. The bamboo floors and light-gray walls added to the sense of space in a shop that was actually fairly small.

William, one of the owners, was standing behind the glass counter at the back. In his fifties, William was small and slim, his hair an everchanging shade of one blonde or another. No other customers were in the shop at the moment, and he was looking at something on his phone. He looked up as they entered the store, and then looked over his shoulder.

"Robert, the little sheriff is here," he called.

"I'm coming," his partner called from a back room.

"Hi, William," Maggie said. "Do you know my mom?"

"No! Hello," he said, and held out a hand.

Georgia took it, and smiled. "Georgia," she said.

"William. With a 'W.' Delighted." He let go of Georgia's hand as Robert came out front. Robert was slightly younger and a great deal taller than William, with almost black hair that he kept slicked back.

"This is your mother?" Robert asked.

"Yes," Maggie answered. "I have one."

"Well. I'm Robert. Welcome."

"Thank you," Georgia replied.

"Mom's here to help me with the flowers," Maggie said.

"Oh, good!" William said, sounding relieved. "Robert, go get the gardenias."

"Gardenias? How nice," Georgia said.

William raised his eyebrows at her and nodded in agreement as Robert went back around the corner. "Of course, they're impossible to find up here this early, but the lady that bought our shop in Fort Lauderdale has some."

"Are they expensive then?" Maggie asked. He waved her question away like she was only auditing his class.

"Look at these gorgeous things!" Robert said as he came back out front. He carried a small handful of brilliant white gardenias wrapped in a damp towel. Maggie could smell them already.

"Oh, those are so pretty," Georgia said. She looked at Maggie. "Do you remember the big gardenia bush my mother had?"

"Yeah," Maggie said, leaning over to sniff. The smell was intoxicating. She wanted to lie down in it. She'd only had one cup of coffee at home, and she could feel some of her circuits shorting out.

"I told you!" William said to Maggie triumphantly. "Gardenias, not roses. Roses are for prom."

"Gardenias are simple, but more modern," Robert said.

"They smell better, too," Georgia said. She looked at Maggie. "Do you like them?"

"Yes. They're beautiful. Really."

"Robert, go do up the bouquet we talked about," William said, then turned to Maggie. "You'll like this. Full, but not fluffy."

No fluff," Robert said. "We told her that. I'll be right back," Robert said.

William looked at Georgia. "Your daughter said that the other ones were too fluffy." He turned his gaze on Maggie. "Table arrangements," he said, slapping the counter a few times.

"You know, it's a potluck," Maggie said hesitantly. "In my parents' back yard."

"It's a wedding," he said firmly. "We're not talking huge, elaborate arrangements here, just a few small arrangements to spiff things up. Maybe a few simple white bowls of gardenias and some greenery."

"You know what would be nice for those?" Robert called from the back. "Silver Dollar Eucalyptus. For length."

"Width," William whispered to Georgia.

Georgia smiled at Maggie. Maggie sighed.

"You know what Mom? I need some more coffee. I'm going to run around the corner and get a latte."

"Okay, sweetie. "

"Do you want anything?" Maggie asked her.

"No, I had plenty," Georgia answered. "William, do you have a restroom I can use?"

"Straight back and to the end."

Georgia smiled and went down the hall.

Maggie looked at William as the bell over the door jangled. "Anything she likes, I'll like."

Two women approached the counter, one a large, blonde woman wearing regrettable heels, the other a smaller, dark-haired woman.

"Hello," William sang out. "I'll be right with you."

"The gardenias are great. Really. I'll be back."

"We'll be here," William said.

Maggie smiled politely at the two women behind her as she headed for the door. The blonde woman watched her go, then turned to Robert. "Hello, I'm Regina Waxler," she said. "I ordered the Hummingbird Bouquet?"

"Oh, yes," William said. "We've got it right here. Robert, can you run that Hummingbird out here real quick?"

"One sec," he called back.

"Wasn't that Maggie Drummond that just left?" Regina asked.

"Oh, yes," William answered. "We're doing her wedding."

Robert came out with a small arrangement of flowers in a green vase. "Here we go," he said, as he came to stand beside William.

"Oh, this is very pretty," Regina said, as she took the vase from Robert. She smiled back up at William. "So that's actually taking place? My goodness."

The little brown-haired lady spoke up quietly. "Regina," she said.

"What? I'm just surprised." She looked back at William and spoke more quietly. "I mean, everybody knows she's been going around with Bennett Boudreaux. She's either seeing him or working for him."

William was about to say something when, out of the corner of his eye, he saw Georgia slowly walk out from the hall, drying her hands on a paper towel.

"I'm just saying," Regina said.

"But you're not saying it while my daughter's still in the shop," Georgia said politely.

William tapped Robert's side. "Get the mister," he whispered.

Regina had enough sense to look embarrassed. Her friend just looked like she wished she had different friends,

"Well, I'm very sorry," Regina said, "I was just repeat—"

"Mr. Boudreaux is not Maggie's lover or her employer," Georgia said. "He's her father. If you're going to spread gossip about other people's private lives, at least make it true." She grabbed her purse from the counter. "Gentlemen, the flowers are beautiful. Please tell Maggie I'm going to walk to Riverfront Park for some fresh air."

Everyone watched her walk to the door, graceful and unhurried. Once the door had closed behind her, the blond woman let out a breath and turned to William. "Those are very nice," she said. She took a wallet out of her purse.

"$49.99," William said stiffly.

"What? You said $29.99 on the phone."

"Well, but then we met," William said.

"What?"

"$49.99," William repeated.

The woman looked at the arrangement and gave William a dirty look. "Forget it. They're not worth fifty dollars."

William picked up a pair of floral shears and started snapping at the flowers, beheading several blossoms.

"Hey," Robert said quietly, as several buds fell to the floor.

"Now they're not worth fifty dollars," William said to the blond woman.

"Come on, Susan," Regina said, and slammed the vase down on the counter. William and Robert watched them leave, William still holding the shears.

Once the door slammed shut, Robert slapped William's shoulder with what was left of the bouquet. "Stupidhead!"

"She was not nice," William said.

"I don't care," Robert said. "We're out fifteen dollars' worth of materials. Next time, just stab her."

"Stabbing's bad for business," William said pertly.

When Maggie walked back into the shop a few minutes later, William looked like he was standing guard at the counter. Robert heard the bell and hurried out from the back. When Maggie got to the counter they were both standing there looking like mismatched toy soldiers.

"Hey, guys," Maggie said, glancing around the shop. "Where's Mom?"

"There was an incident," William answered.

"An altercation," Robert clarified.

"She said to tell you she would be at Riverfront Park," William added.

Maggie gave them a nervous grin. "You guys, what did you do to my mother?"

"Not us. The hag," William said.

"What hag? Those ladies that were just here?"

"The *zaftig* one," Robert answered.

As far as Maggie knew, her mother had never been in an altercation with anyone. "What happened?"

"That woman was talking trash about you," William said.

"What do you mean?"

"About you and Bennett Boudreaux," Robert said, and Maggie felt a swirling in her stomach.

"Your mom came out from the ladies' room and heard," William explained.

"Oh, crap," Maggie said quietly.

"Your Mom set her straight," William said proudly.

"But like a lady," Robert said.

Maggie swallowed. "What did she say?"

"Oh." William said, straightening his shoulders. "Well."

"Not our affair," Robert said.

Maggie blew out a breath and smiled. "It's okay. I know what she said."

⚓ ⚓ ⚓

Georgia was standing at the edge of the dock that fronted Riverfront Park. It was breezy there, and she hugged her sweater around her as her long, dark hair swirled around her face.

"Mom?"

Georgia looked over her shoulder, tried for a smile, then turned to face her daughter. "Maggie, I'm sorry."

Maggie stopped in front of her. "Why?"

"Because it wasn't my place to tell it."

"I don't really care anymore," Maggie said. She shrugged one shoulder. "If the kids didn't know, it would be different."

Georgia sighed. "It's just...one of the biggest reasons we kept it a secret back then is because I had this stupid fear of people talking about me, of people gossiping about what 'good little Georgia' did. The choir girl and the daughter of the Chief of Police. It was the seventies and it was stupid because nobody really would have cared, except your grandfather."

"It's okay, Mom," Maggie said.

"It's just...I stood there listening to what she said, and I realized that people were saying the same things about you that I had been afraid they'd say about me, and I got so angry."

Maggie reached out and took her mother's chilled hand.

"Mom, it really doesn't matter to me, if people know." She tried a smile. "At least nobody's going to think I'm sleeping with him anymore."

Georgia looked her in the eye for a moment. "I'm sorry about...the whole thing, Maggie. Sorry it happened, and sorry we kept it from you for so long."

Maggie thought about how hurt she'd been when she found out, how angry she was that her mother had been unfaithful, how indignant she was that she had been lied to. But then she thought about Sky and Kyle, and how devastating it would be to be separated from them in any way, how badly she would need their forgiveness if she hurt them.

She opened her mouth to say something, but then couldn't think of what that should be. So, she wrapped her arms around her mother, felt Georgia's arms enfold her, and let that be enough said.

CHAPTER

SIXTEEN

illiam Newcombe turned out to be a bust or, more accurately, the lack of one. He'd been home when Wyatt and Maggie got there, and it turned out that he did have a job. He'd just started working on one of the shrimp boats, and they'd been out since yesterday afternoon. He claimed he'd been working Wednesday night, too, and when Maggie called Lyle Spencer, a shrimper she'd known her whole life, he confirmed it.

The last person on their list was Bobby Farley. He lived just north of Avenue L on 24th Avenue, and Maggie stopped at the Marathon to gas up the Jeep and let Wyatt grab a Mountain Dew. Then they headed up 98, which in that part of town was basically considered Avenue E, or Main Street, depending on who was giving the directions.

They had just turned right onto 24th, heading north, when they saw a large, navy blue Ford F-150 coming their way. "That our guy right there?" Wyatt asked.

They looked over as the truck passed. The driver was a man in his early thirties or so, with dark brown hair that touched his collar.

"Let's go see," Maggie said. She checked the road, which was stick-straight, and clear for quite a way, then she slowly turned the Jeep around to follow. They were about halfway to caught up when the pickup suddenly increased its speed.

"There he goes, Wyatt said.

Maggie sped up, as well, while Wyatt turned on her dashboard light. Maggie caught up to the truck, and when she saw the driver checking his rear view, she stuck out her hand and pointed to the right side of the road. He looked back at the road and slammed on the gas.

So did Maggie, and she followed his right turn onto Brownsville Road.

Wyatt picked up Maggie's radio. "Franklin-101 to Franklin, be advised we are 10-31 of a dark blue in color pickup, with tag number Oscar Lima 59 Bravo 3. Attempting to 10-50 on Brownsville Road, headed westbound."

Maggie's radio squawked back and they heard one of the female dispatchers respond.

"10-26 Franklin-101. All units 10-33 traffic." This let the other officers know that only traffic emergencies would take precedence over joining the chase.

Wyatt replaced the radio and looked at Maggie. "Maybe he's late picking his mother up at the airport."

The Apalachicola Municipal airport didn't bring too many mothers to town. It served small charters and cargo planes mostly, and a few puddle jumpers from Tallahassee and Panama City.

They listened as first one, then another officer from Apalach PD advised that they were en route.

"Coming up on the traffic circle," Wyatt said.

"I've done this before, too."

"Don't be snotty."

As they approached the traffic circle, Maggie saw that a dump truck carrying dirt or mulch was about to make a right onto Brownsville, and that, to their right, a blue sedan was pulling into the traffic circle from the westbound side of Pal Rivers Road.

"Crap," Maggie said, as the pickup barreled on without slowing.

The driver ignored the fact that he was only supposed to go right on the traffic circle. Instead, he bore left to avoid the sedan, driving directly across the large median in the center.

The bottom of the pickup slammed back down onto the eastbound side of Pal Rivers Road with a metallic groan. The driver veered to the left a bit, then overcorrected as he swung to the right. Maggie went right in the circle, followed it around, and was pulling onto Pal

Rivers when the truck swung back to the left, over the median, and blew out the left front tire.

Wyatt picked up and keyed the radio. "Franklin 101 to Franklin. Be advised subject truck is now northbound on Pal Rivers Road."

"10-26 Franklin 101." The dispatcher went on to advise the responding officers from PD.

The pickup continued for about a hundred yards, then swerved left into the sandy median. The driver scrambled out, across the median and then the opposite lane. There was a good fifty yards of open land, then nothing but woods.

"Crap," Maggie said, as she slowed enough to pull onto the right shoulder. Wyatt picked up the radio.

"Franklin 101 to Franklin. Suspect vehicle is S-4 in median just past traffic circle."

Maggie hurriedly unbuckled her seat belt, and Wyatt followed suit and opened his door. "Subject is fleeing on foot," Wyatt continued, as Maggie jumped out of the Jeep. "Myself and Franklin 103 are in pursuit on foot. Please have all available units en route, and call Franklin CI and request Officer Chisholm to be en route with the bloodhounds."

Maggie was across the road before Wyatt started running. The man they assumed was Bobby Trainer was just making the woods. Maggie pulled her Glock from her back holster and ran harder. It could take a good half hour for the bloodhounds to get there, depending on where in the county they were. By that time, this guy would be gone.

Maggie hit the woods about thirty seconds after Trainer did. The area was an obstructive mix of tall brush and young trees. Maggie could hear Trainer better than she could see him. He veered to the right as she heard Wyatt come in behind and a little to the right of her position.

"Bobby Trainer, stop!" Maggie yelled.

She heard a great deal of rustling followed by a grunt, then she caught a glimpse of him scrambling from the ground, about twenty feet ahead and right. A thin branch with unkind foliage slapped her in the face as she went through. Her right eye stung and tried to shut. She blinked rapidly as her eye watered, then cut to the right. Wyatt suddenly flew past her on the right, and a few seconds later, they hit a less-wooded patch. Wyatt closed the distance between him and Trainer, and tackled him to the ground.

Trainer let out an angry yell and struggled to get Wyatt off him as Maggie caught up. She pointed her weapon at him. "Don't do that," she said. He looked at her gun, then looked her in the eye, and stopped struggling. Maggie tossed Wyatt her cuffs, and he sat up on Trainer's legs and pulled his wrists back.

"Awful lot of trouble to avoid a speeding ticket," Wyatt said.

Trainer tried to look over his shoulder at Wyatt, then looked at Maggie, shock and confusion on his voice.

"What?" he blurted.

Maggie heard running steps behind and to the left of them. "Over here!" she yelled.

Wyatt finished cuffing Trainer and stood up, his breathing just a little bit rough. He shook out his right hand and wiggled his index finger, as Jack Linder from Apalach PD ran into the clearing.

"We're all good," Wyatt told him.

"That wasn't much of a foot pursuit," Linder said, grinning.

"He's not much of a runner," Wyatt said, as he pulled Trainer to his feet. "Are you Bobby Trainer?" he asked him.

Wyatt turned Trainer around and started walking him back the way they'd come. Maggie and Linder fell in step behind him.

"Why?"

"Come on, you've got ID, I'm sure."

Maggie and Linder used their hands to push branches out of their way. Wyatt used Bobby Trainer.

Trainer tried to look indignant. "Yeah, I'm Bobby Trainer."

"Then Bobby Trainer, you are under arrest for evading an officer and reckless driving," Wyatt said. "We'll talk about the other stuff later, when I have some Mountain Dew."

"What other stuff?" Trainer asked, but Wyatt's only answer was to Mirandize him.

Once they got to the clear area, Maggie pulled off her radio and keyed it. "Franklin 101 to Franklin."

"Franklin to Franklin 103, go ahead."

"Subject is in custody. Myself and Franklin 101 will be 10-51 to Franklin County Jail with one white male 10-15."

"10-26, Franklin 103. 10-51 one white male 10-15."

As the little group reached the road, a small red pickup with a camper top pulled over behind Maggie's Jeep. As they crossed the road, Officer Shawn Chisholm, from Franklin Correctional, jumped out of the truck. He was a slim, twenty-something young man with lots of teeth, a high forehead, and a wide smile.

"Aw, man. Is that your guy?" Chisholm asked.

"Yeah," Maggie answered. "How'd you get here so fast?"

"It's my day off," he said. "Well, dang. What am I supposed to tell Cash and Suzy Q? They were pretty excited."

"Sorry, Shawn," Wyatt said. "We'll give the next guy a better head start."

Since Wyatt and Maggie weren't in a cruiser, Officer Linder transported Bobby Trainer to the SO for them. The jail was accessed through a separate entrance, and Wyatt and Maggie walked Trainer through, and left Dwight to get him booked and settled into an interview room.

Then they entered the wing where the SO was housed, and headed for the break room.

They met Burt coming their way.

"Hey, Burt, where's the sheriff?" Wyatt asked as they got closer.

"He's over at that county commissioners' thing or whatever," Burt answered. "Should be back pretty soon, though." "Thanks," Wyatt said, as he and Maggie turned into the break room.

Wyatt pulled a big bottle of Mountain Dew from his stash in the fridge, and handed Maggie a bottled water.

"How are you going to go at this guy?" Wyatt asked.

Maggie took a long swallow of her water. It was cold and sweet, and she hadn't realized she was so thirsty.

"Actually, I was thinking you should take him," she said.

"Why?"

Maggie shrugged a little. "He strikes me as one of those guys who doesn't want to talk to a woman unless he's hitting on her. Either he won't take me seriously enough or he'll get too defensive."

"Okay," Wyatt said. "This guy isn't much of an intellectual, but I don't think even he's dumb enough to run just because we tried to pull him over. He was there."

"Maybe he's been doing something we don't know about and thinks that's why we came after him."

"Maybe, but not likely."

"No."

"I think he was there. Whether he was a witness or our guy, I don't know, but either way, he's scared, and that's how we like 'em."

SEVENTEEN

When Wyatt and Maggie joined him in the interview room, at just past 9am, Bobby Trainer was nervously tapping on the scarred wooden table, looking like he had someplace he needed to be.

Maggie pulled her notepad and pen from her pocket, and took an uncomfortable seat across the table. Wyatt leaned against the wall behind her.

"Why'd you take off, Bobby?" he asked.

Trainer blinked a couple of times. "Why'd you try to pull me over?"

"I asked you first," Wyatt said.

"I done time," Trainer said. "You guys pull a U-ey and come after me with your lights, so I panicked."

"Well, gee, Bobby, we just needed your help with something."

Trainer thought about that for a moment. Maggie swore she could hear the gears squeaking.

"What do you mean?" Trainer asked finally.

"Well, see, we're looking for a truck like yours, on account of this case we're working," Wyatt said amiably. "See, the truck was seen leaving a murder scene—"

"A what?" Trainer yelped.

"Yeah, a murder scene, and so we figure the driver might be a witness, and might be able to help us out."

"I don't know what you're talking about!"

"But out of all the other trucks like yours in town, you're the only driver that took off and made us chase him through the woods. And you know what that tells us, right?"

"No."

"Well, since you didn't have any meth or dead bodies in your truck, it tells us that you had some other really compelling reason to not want to talk to us."

"No, it don't."

"It does," Wyatt said. "So why don't you talk to us about Lake Morality."

"What? What about it?" Trainer shifted in his seat.

"Don't jerk me around, Bobby," Wyatt said, the friendliness gone from his voice.

Trainer's eyes darted around, like he was looking for a door they'd left open.

"I don't want to say nothin' else," Trainer said.

"That's your prerogative, Bobby, but now that we have your truck, we can match your tires to the treads we took from the lake."

That was untrue. They hadn't gotten any decent treads. But Wyatt was so convincing that Maggie almost wondered why nobody had told her.

"No. I wasn't there," Trainer said.

"Your truck was," Wyatt said. "And it was there at 11pm Wednesday night, right around the time somebody drowned a young mother."

"Aw, crap, man!" Trainer started to stand up, forgetting that his cuffs were attached to the table. "No, man, Uh-uh," he blurted. "No."

He sat back down in his little plastic chair.

"Calm down, Bobby," Wyatt said. "We might be able to help you a little bit if you just tell us what happened."

"I don't know what happened, man!" Trainer actually looked like he might cry.

"Why? Did you black out? Were you really drunk or high?"

"No, man. I wasn't there!"

"What do you want to tell me, Bobby? Wyatt asked quietly.

Trainer looked up at Wyatt. He looked lost, like he'd thought it would be fun to run away from his mother at the mall, but now he couldn't find her. Maggie would have felt sorry for him if he wasn't a creep.

"Look, man, I didn't do anything, I promise you!" Trainer said. "I just loaned him my truck. I've never killed no one! I don't even get in fights, man."

"Who borrowed your truck?" Wyatt asked.

Maggie clicked her pen open, while Trainer stared at nothing on the table. Wyatt said nothing, let the silence become more and more uncomfortable.

"A guy I was in with," Trainer finally said.

"What's his name?"

"Listen, man—Sheriff—you gotta understand. He's kind of a scary guy," Trainer said. "I go back in and he goes back in, it's not looking good for me."

"Listen, Bobby," Wyatt said smoothly. "You tell us who he is and tell us what happened, you might not even do any time. A little reckless driving, some speeding, we might be able to work with that. If you don't help us out, I promise you'll be back in Franklin with a quickness."

Trainer thought about that for a minute. Maggie clicked her pen open and shut several times to help him think.

"Curt Shook," Trainer said to the table.

"Spell it," Maggie said. He did, and she wrote it down, and started texting Dwight to run the name.

"Talk to me about Shook," Wyatt said. "What was the deal?"

"Look, you just—you gotta understand, I don't know anything about Lake Morality. He didn't tell me anything."

"Explain it to me," Wyatt said.

"Okay, see, the original plan was he needed me to pick him up from Lake Morality Tuesday night. He was gonna call me and tell me when."

"Tuesday night?" Maggie asked.

"Yeah," Trainer answered, but he said it to Wyatt.

"Okay," Wyatt prompted.

"I asked him what the hell he needed me to get him from the lake for, because he has a car, you know? But he said I didn't need to know, that it was better I didn't."

"So, what happened Tuesday?"

"So, he calls me Tuesday afternoon, like three or four—I was still at work—and he says there's a change of plans. He says he doesn't need me. So, I say okay."

"Okay, so then what happened?" Wyatt asked. "How'd he end up with your truck Wednesday night?"

"He calls me up Wednesday, like six o' clock, somewhere around there, and he says he needs the truck. He wants to borrow it." Trainer sat up straighter in his chair. "I don't want to, you know, but I'm telling you, this guy's cold. If he hadn't decided to be my friend in County, he would have been one of my biggest fears, you know?"

"Okay," Wyatt said.

"So, I ask him what's going on and he won't tell me. Starts getting all wired up. He says his car won't start and he needs the truck. He tells me to bring the it over to his house. He's got a house like a few blocks down from me. He tells me drop off the truck and go home, and he'll have it back to me in a couple of hours."

"What's the address?" Maggie asked.

Trainer looked up at the ceiling. "Uh, 1420. The blue trim."

"So, you took him the truck," Wyatt said.

"Yeah."

"Was anybody with him? Did you go inside the house?"

"No, I didn't go in. I wasn't invited and I didn't want to anyway. I don't know if he had anybody there."

"Where was he taking the truck?" Wyatt asked.

"That was my question, but he tells me I'm better off if I don't know, that he doesn't want to get me into a bad situation."

"Okay," Wyatt said.

"So, I got kind of agitated because he wanted to take my truck. That's my truck, you know? I told him I wanted to help him out, cause I don't want him mad at me, right? But I needed to know what was going on."

"So he told you what?"

"He told me nothin' man," Trainer said. "He pulls this .45 out of the back of his pants and starts telling me I got no loyalty, that I don't appreciate stuff he done for me back inside."

"Keep talking," Wyatt said.

"Well, I'm scared, you know? I mean, I'm pretty sure he's not gonna go shooting me right in his front yard, but he's got a gun, you know? I was scared."

"I get it, you were scared," Wyatt said. "I'd be scared, too."

"Right?" Trainer said. "So I told him I was sorry, that I wasn't trying to be ungrateful, I just really like my truck."

"So, what did he say?"

"He calms down after a minute, and he says he just needs the truck for a couple of hours and nothing's gonna happen to it." Trainer shrugged. "Tells me he'll give me a thousand bucks for loaning it. So, I gave him the keys."

"Then what?"

"Then I walk my ass over to my next-door neighbors', 'cause they're having a party, and I'd rather get slapped for a parole violation than be without some kind of alibi while Curt's got my truck."

"When did he bring the truck back?"

"I don't know. I didn't hear it. But when I looked over there around midnight, it was there."

"So, did he ever come pay you the thousand bucks?"

"It was in the visor, with my keys. Cash."

Dwight's face appeared in the little glass window in the door, and Maggie stood up.

"We'll be back in a minute, Bobby," Wyatt said.

Wyatt held the door open for Maggie, then followed her out and closed it.

"What have you got, Dwight?" Maggie asked.

Dwight handed her a copy of the printout, then read from his own.

"Okay, so this guy Shook did a year from 2007 to 2008 for assault and violation of a court order," Dwight read. "Then he went in for another seven from 2010 to last year for especially aggravated battery. His girlfriend. He hurt her pretty bad."

"When was Trainer in Franklin?" Maggie asked.

"Felony possession, 2014 to 2016," Dwight said.

"Okay, do me a favor, ask Burt to come deal with Trainer," Maggie said. "Then let's figure out where we want to go with Shook."

Dwight walked off in the direction of the deputies' offices.

"What do you think?" Maggie asked Wyatt.

"I think Bobby's right. He sounds like a scary guy."

He opened the door and walked back into the interview room, held the door for Maggie.

"Okay, Bobby, we're going to go file our reports. Officer Simpson is going to come in and take your statement, get you booked."

"Well, I need to call my lawyer," Trainer said. "When do I get my call?"

"You'll get your call when I'm done with my report," Wyatt said. He held his hand and wiggled his index finger. "But, I only type with two fingers, and I think you broke this one."

EIGHTEEN

Maggie, Dwight, and Wyatt were sitting around the conference room table. During the last hour or so, the clouds had gotten lower and looked swollen with rain. The light through the large picture window had a gray tint to it, and Maggie watched as the hibiscus bushes outside did a spastic little dance in the breeze.

Wyatt looked at his watch. "Is he coming, or what?"

"Burt said he saw him pull in," Dwight said. "Reckon he had to pee."

Just then, the door swung open and Bledsoe came in, a file folder in hand. "All right, so what's the plan here?"

He sat down in the chair at the head of the table closest to the door. The rest of the group was all the way down at the other end.

"Did you read Trainer's statement?" Wyatt asked.

"Yeah. Are we buying it?"

"I think he told us the truth as he knows it," Wyatt said.

"Trainer's not the fastest rat in the maze," Maggie said." I can't see somebody like Curt Shook giving this guy any more information than he had to."

"But, originally, he told Trainer to pick him up Tuesday night," Bledsoe said. "He had to know this guy was gonna put it together once the murder got out."

"Yeah, that's true," Wyatt said. "But if I was Shook, I'd rather take the risk Trainer's going to suspect something. From his perspective, who cares if another felon, in particular a frightened felon, suspects he might have done something out at the lake?"

"I can see that," Bledsoe said. "So, what's going on with this DNA?"

"Shook's DNA is in the system. It was used as evidence in this especially aggravated he was in for," said Wyatt. "Apparently, the girlfriend managed to stab him in the hand with a fork."

"Larry's seeing if it matches the DNA from under Kristen's nails," Maggie said. "He said he'd get back to us in a couple of hours at the most, so we should hear from him soon."

"So what are we thinking for motive?" Bledsoe asked. "Kidnap for ransom that went bad somehow?"

"We thought about that," Wyatt said. "But the theory has issues."

"What are those?" Bledsoe asked him.

"Well, for one thing, as far as we know, Morgan never got a ransom call," Maggie answered.

"Kidnappers always tell the families not to call the police," Bledsoe said. "He might have gotten a call and not told us about it."

"He might have," Wyatt said. "And if he paid the money, or even couldn't pay the money, and his wife is dead, he might not ever want to tell us there was contact."

"Maybe he paid it, and Shook killed her anyway," Maggie said. "Or maybe something went wrong, and he killed her."

"Well, seems to me something went wrong," Bledsoe said, looking down at the file. "I mean, he arranged for this dimwit to pick him up from Lake Morality Tuesday night, but he doesn't kill her till Wednesday night. So, what do we make of that?"

"If it *was* a kidnap for ransom, maybe Morgan couldn't pay, or couldn't pay right away," Wyatt said. "But that leaves lots of holes."

"If he was supposed to take her in her own car, what was he planning to do with the baby?" Maggie asked. "If he was on the the street, or even just across the parking lot, he saw her put Ellie in the car."

"Maybe he wanted both of them, but she screwed that up for him by locking him out," Bledsoe said.

"Yeah, but if it was a kidnap, and he did make contact with Morgan, would Morgan really keep that from the rest of the family?" Wyatt asked. "Would he even be able to?"

"Yeah," Dwight said. "That doesn't seem real likely. Not unless he said he couldn't pay it and then she got killed. Maybe he would want to keep it a secret then."

"Well, maybe this guy was a really inexpensive kidnapper, but I can't see courting life without parole for anything less than a few hundred-thousand, and Morgan doesn't have it," Wyatt said. "He's not hurting, but he doesn't have much in the way of liquid assets."

"We thought about the possibility that this was a straight-up hit, that it was supposed to look like a kidnapping gone bad, or even suicide, but that Morgan was behind it," Maggie said.

"But he's only got a $250,000 policy on her," Wyatt said. "He's just not hurting enough to need that, not when it could go all wrong and land him in prison."

"Then why take her?" Bledsoe asked. "Because she drove an Escalade? So does every other drug dealer. Doesn't mean she's rich."

"We need to just go get this guy and ask him," Maggie said.

"I agree," Bledsoe said. "SWAT's tied up all the way up in Tate's Hell, on that meth bust. But Apalach PD has two guys they can send with us, and you can take Burt and Myles. That makes seven officers."

Maggie did the math in her head. Bledsoe wouldn't be going with them.

"PD did a drive-by," Wyatt said. "They said Shook's car is there, but they didn't see anyone. Even so, we'll assume he's there and we know he's armed."

"Who's taking the lead?" Bledsoe asked.

Maggie wanted to ask him why he wasn't. "Wyatt," she said instead. She looked at Wyatt. "You've staged a lot more of these than I have."

"Okay, then let's get Myles and Burt in here, and let's figure how to grab this guy without screwing it up," Wyatt said. "It's only 10:30. Maybe we'll have this wrapped up in time for dinner."

Just then the phone in the center of the table rang. Wyatt was closest, so he picked it up.

"Hey, Burt," he said, then listened for a moment. "Thanks."

Wyatt hung up the phone and looked at Maggie. "Larry's got a match. Shook's our guy."

⚓   ⚓   ⚓

William Shook's house was two houses from the corner. It was a white house of CBS construction, circa 1960, with royal blue trim better suited for a boat. It was a shady lot, as many of the lots on 24th Avenue were, thanks to a plentiful number of mature pines.

The wooded lot behind Shook's was undeveloped and offered even more cover, so that was where everyone convened. The house beside it was empty and for sale, and Maggie's Jeep and Dwight's cruiser parked in its driveway. Burt had ridden with Dwight. Myles had been called to a domestic issue on 22nd St, but they decided to go with what they had.

The three of them were checking their body armor and testing their headsets and radio mics when Wyatt and two officers from PD pulled in. Richard Chase and Jack Linder exited Chase's cruiser, wearing their own body armor over their black uniforms. Wyatt climbed out of his truck and the three men approached Maggie's group.

It had been a while since Maggie had seen Wyatt wearing a vest, or needing to, and she swallowed hard as he reached her.

"Okay, when I drove by, the car was still sitting in the yard," Wyatt said. "Maybe it doesn't run, maybe it does. Let's assume he's home either way." He ran his eyes over Maggie. She knew he was mentally tightening the Velcro straps of her vest, even though they couldn't get any tighter.

"So here's the deal," Wyatt continued. "Richard, Jack and I are going to pull our vehicles right up into his driveway, nice and calm. It'll either hold his attention for a minute so you guys can move into place, or he'll bolt right away. Unless he's got a side door we can't see, he'll come out the back."

"Might be good to single-file it along that tree line by his fence," Maggie said.

"I agree," Wyatt said. "The less time you guys spend running across his yard, the happier I'll be."

They ran through a radio check one more time, then Wyatt stepped over and gave Maggie a quick, but strong, squeeze. "Not that I don;t love you guys, too," Wyatt said, unsmiling.

He waved at Richard and Jack to follow him. "Okay, on my go," he said, as they walked to their cars.

Maggie, Dwight and Burt pulled their service weapons, exchanged looks, then Dwight led the way through the trees to the beginning of Shook's back yard. His neighbor to their right had a brown-painted wood fence to mark his property line. Shook had some evergreens to mark his. They had about two feet between them, and the trees took them to within about ten yards of Shook's back door. Ten yards didn't seem like a lot until you needed cover, and there was nothing there but a couple of aluminum folding chairs and a small fire pit that was lying on its side.

Once they got to the corner of Shook's yard, where the tree line started, they all hunkered down to wait for Wyatt's signal. Maggie stared at the back of Dwight's neck and hated that even that much of him was exposed to a bullet. Everyone at the Sheriff's Office was part of her extended family, but Dwight's folks were shrimpers, and had been close friends of her parents most of Maggie's life. Even if he hadn't been painfully skinny and terribly sweet, Maggie would have felt particularly protective of him.

They'd been crouched there for about two minutes when Wyatt 's calm voice came through their headsets. "Take your positions."

The three of them duckwalked as fast as possible along the tree line, as Maggie heard Wyatt knock on the door. "Curt Shook. Franklin County Sheriff's Office," he said through her headset.

Maggie kept her eyes on the back of the house as she followed closely on Dwight's heels. There was no sign of anyone, but that meant little. They broke from the tree line and rushed to the back door, as Wyatt called Curt Shook once more. There was a small open porch with three concrete steps. Dwight and Maggie split at the door, with her on the right and Dwight on the left. Burt was one step below Dwight and on his side.

"Go!" They heard from Wyatt, and Dwight checked the knob. It was locked. Two seconds later, Burt kicked it open and he and Dwight went in together as they heard the front door slam open.

Dwight and Burt split to the left and right of a kitchen straight out of the seventies. "Maggie," Dwight said, and she followed them in. They swept the area with their guns as they heard Wyatt and his team enter the house. Burt checked a utility room to the right, Dwight swept his weapon to the left. Maggie went down the center to a swinging door in the wall.

She heard one of the men in front move down a hallway to her left, and then another. She heard more movement behind her as Burt approached and took the other side of the swinging door.

"Clear," she heard Richard say after a moment. Wyatt and Jack repeated it.

Maggie stood, and lowered her service weapon. "We're clear," she called out, and she and her guys moved through the swinging door to a wide living room.

Richard and Chase were coming out of the hallway. Wyatt came back to the living room from an open door on the right. Maggie could just see the corner of a dresser behind him.

"Nothing," Wyatt said.

Everyone sighed or caught their breath. The adrenaline that had been coursing through Maggie's veins didn't know yet that the danger was over, so her heart pounded and her mouth felt dry. She holstered her weapon as they all looked around.

"Cozy," Dwight said.

Maggie nodded. The curtains were drawn against the sunlight, and the room would have felt dreary even without the brown plaid couch and the stained green carpet.

"Jack and Richard," Wyatt said. "I need you to take the cruiser and my truck, get them out of the yard. Take either end of the block, and keep an eye out for our guy in case he just went out to The Pig for some pickles."

"Gotcha," Jack said as he caught Wyatt's keys.

He and Richard checked the front yard before going out. They closed the door behind them, though the trim was splintered and the plate was bent.

Wyatt walked back toward the bedroom on Maggie's right. She looked at Dwight as she pulled a pair of blue Latex gloves from her front jeans pocket.

"Can you and Burt go ahead and look around the kitchen, and that laundry room? "I'll start back there," she said, jerking her thumb at the hallway.

"Okay," Dwight said, pulling his own pair of gloves from his back pocket.

Maggie made her way down the dark hall. The house was bigger than it seemed from the outside, but the oppressive darkness made it feel closed in and claustrophobic. The first room on the left side of the hall looked like it was meant to be a bedroom, but it was clearly just for storage. There were several pieces of furniture and a collection of cardboard boxes and plastic totes. Piled onto an old dresser were towers of books and VHS tapes.

A check on Shook's property had revealed that the house had been owned by his mother, who had passed away in 2013. It had been paid off several years prior to Shook inheriting, but several months ago, he had taken out a $60,000 mortgage. It didn't look like he'd done any remodeling, so they wondered what the heck he'd done with the money.

The room across the hall was another, smaller bedroom. The only furniture was a twin iron bed with a bare mattress and chipped white paint, a small fake wood night-stand, and a small upholstered chair in one corner. In another corner was a pile of fishing gear, including four poles leaning against the wall.

In here, as in the rest of the house that Maggie had seen, there were heavy curtains pulled shut over the windows. These were avocado green with white flowers, in a heavy fabric that looked like damask. Maggie used a finger to pull one curtain aside. A huge hibiscus blocked the view of the side yard almost completely.

She dropped the curtain and walked over to the night-stand. Opening the slightly warped drawer revealed a few rusted bobby pins, a brochure for a restaurant that had been closed for several years, and half a box of tissues.

Maggie closed the drawer again and turned her atten-tion to the bed. It would have been a beautiful little bed if it hadn't been in the home of a killer. Maggie had found that no matter how nice a place was, no matter how clean, if it belonged to someone who had done something ter-rible, it all seemed tainted and diseased.

Maggie spotted a tiny bit of red mixed in with the chipped white paint on one of the rails, and she found her flashlight app, turned it on, and tried to lean in without letting any part of herself come into contact with the bed.

At first glance, she had thought it might be blood, but once she got closer, she saw that it was some type of fibers that had caught on the chipped paint. They were short and somewhat frizzy. Could be from a blanket or pillow case but could be something else. Maggie straightened up and keyed her shoulder mic.

"Hey Burt, could you grab my kit out of the back of my Jeep?"

"Yeah. Got something?"

"Maybe, maybe not, but I'm not leaving it."

"Okay, be right there," he answered.

Maggie looked underneath the bed but found nothing but dust bunnies and an old fishing magazine. She straightened back up, and went back out to the hall. The only room left was a small bathroom at the end of the hall. It didn't look like it got much use. There was no bath mat, there were no towels on the racks, no toothbrush in the toothbrush holder on the wall. Either this guy never bathed, or there was another bathroom on the other side of the house.

She opened the medicine cabinet. There was a toothbrush still in the package, and what looked to be a pretty old disposable razor. The blade was completely rusted. Opening the vanity door, she found a moldy water stain beneath the drain pipe, and nothing else.

She stood back up and looked behind the dolphin-themed shower curtain. The grout was gray with dirt and age. A thin coat of dust covered the bottom and sides of the tub.

"Hey, here's your kit, Mags," Burt said behind her. She turned around.

"Thanks," she said. "Can you just put it inside that bedroom door right there?" Burt gave her a thumbs-up and turned to go. "Have you found anything interesting?" she asked him.

"Not really. I can tell you the guy eats pretty good," he said over his shoulder. "Somebody around here likes to cook. All kinds of fancy food in the fridge, and about a hundred cookbooks in the pantry. But nobody's real big on doing the dishes."

"Any sign that he's been cooking for two lately?"

"Not that I see."

Maggie lifted the cover from the toilet tank and peeked inside, more out of habit than anything else. There was nothing there but rusty water.

She had just stepped back into the hall when Wyatt appeared at the end of it. "What did you find?" he asked her as he walked toward her.

Maggie shook her head. "Not much. How about you?"

"His bedroom's the master off the living room. No sign of any female companions, but he likes porn and sex toys."

"Remind me to throw up later," Maggie said as she walked back into the bedroom. " There are some fibers on this bed in here that interest me," she said, crouching down to open her kit.

"Why?" Wyatt followed her as far as the doorway.

She pulled an evidence bag and a pair of long tweezers from her kit.

"Just because this room looks like it hasn't been used in forever, but it seems like these fibers would have been long gone if that's the case."

"What color fibers?" Wyatt asked from the doorway.

Maggie walked toward the bed. "Red. Reddish."

Wyatt left the doorway, and Maggie pulled several of the small fibers from the iron rail and dropped them into the evidence bag. She was walking back to her kit when Wyatt appeared in the doorway again. He held a pair of red velvet handcuffs on the end of a pen.

"This color?" he asked.

Maggie stopped a few feet away and peered at them. "You think those would leave ligature marks or bruising on a wrist?"

"You're asking me like you suspect me of knowing the answer," he said.

"From professional experience, jerk."

"I have no idea, actually. We can ask Larry. Hand me a bag."

Maggie grabbed a bag for him and held it open. He slid the cuffs in. She held her bag up next to his. If she was betting, she'd bet that the fibers were from the cuffs.

"Can you label that for me? Wyatt asked. "I'm gonna check on Dwight and Burt."

Maggie labelled the two bags and dropped them into her kit. Then she turned around and looked at the little iron bed, at the dingy carpet and the dark curtains.

She saw Kristen there on the bed, alone, terrified and wondering if she would ever see her daughter again. Maggie could almost feel the sadness. The room was suddenly filled with Kristen's hopelessness, and Maggie found herself hoping that when they found Shook, he would resist arrest.

She walked back out to the front of the house. Dwight was poking through a pile of mail on the glass coffee table.

"Where's Wyatt?" she asked.

"Outside," he said. "Neighbor come over."

Maggie could hear muffled voice's out front, one of them Wyatt's and the other belonging to another man. She walked toward the door, but she was only halfway there when Wyatt quickly stepped back in.

"Our guy's doing some freelance painting work," he said. "Neighbor said he talked to him yesterday morning. He's doing some trim paint over at the Water Street Hotel."

"His car's here," Maggie said, though it wasn't that important.

"He's riding a bike."

NINETEEN

They left Jack and Richard stationed in their cars a few blocks down from Shook's house in either direction. Then they called for some replacements to meet Maggie, Dwight, Wyatt and Burt in the large gravel parking lot of the Scipio Creek Marina.

Next to the marina's parking lot was almost an acre of brush, bushes and small trees. On the other side of it was the Water Street Hotel & Marina. The hotel was a three-story stucco structure, painted brick red, with just a few dozen apartment-style rooms. Behind the hotel was a dock with slips for guests arriving by boat.

Pax Brooks from Apalach PD joined them first, and Myles pulled in a few minutes later. Both of them had gone the long way around via Commerce, avoiding Market and Water Streets, where they had a chance of being seen from the hotel.

Once they were all there, everyone gathered around the hood of Maggie's Jeep. Wyatt had grabbed a pen and was drawing on the blank side of a Hong Kong Bistro menu.

"Go ahead and call," Wyatt said. Maggie pulled out her cell and dialed the number for the front desk at Water Street. It was answered on the second ring.

"Water Street Hotel and Marina, this is Linda speaking. How may I help you?"

Maggie immediately felt badly about Linda's day. Linda was a friend; they'd known each other for years through their daughters' softball teams. Linda was from Brooklyn, though her mother was born and raised in Apalach, and despite many years in Apalach, she sounded exactly like a New Yorker. A buxom, curvaceous African-American woman in her fifties, she was funny and warm. Maggie wondered why she never made an effort to see Linda these days.

"Hey, Linda, it's Maggie Redmond."

"Hey, girl, what are you doing?"

"Working a lot," Maggie said. "Listen, I just have a minute, but do you have a guy named Curt Shook doing some work on the hotel?"

"The painter guy? Yeah, why?"

"Is he working now?"

"What's wrong with him?" Linda demanded. "I don't have time for any tomfoolery round here—"

"Don't worry, it's fine," Maggie said. "Is he there?"

"Yeah, do you need me to get him?"

"No, I'll swing by," Maggie answered. "Where on the property is he?"

"I saw him a little while ago in the back," Linda answered, her voice suspicious. "He's painting the railings back there by the dock."

"Okay, thanks, Linda," Maggie said. "Don't mention I called, okay?"

"See, that's how I know—"

Maggie hung up the phone. "He's painting some rails on the ground floor, in back by the docks."

Wyatt put an "X" on the back side of a very rough outline of the hotel.

"Okay. So, Myles and Pax, if you head up the north side of the lot, you'll end up just about on top of that end of the hotel. That'll give you fast access to the back on that end. Burt, you and Dwight cut across the lot and come up behind the pool." He looked at Maggie. "There's a wall there, right?"

"Yeah, topped by a short fence. The pool area is built up."

"Okay, so you guys come up behind the pool, and Dwight you come around this side of it, and Burt you come around this side. That'll put both of you in decent positions if he happens to come around the front, or if he makes it past Myles and Pax."

"What about this whole side, here?" Dwight asked, indicating the small circular drive and the office.

"Maggie has an idea about that," Wyatt answered.

"We're going to drive right up," she said.

She walked around to the back of the Jeep, lifted the gate, and turned over the overnight bag that was still in her cargo area. She unzipped it and rummaged for a moment, then pulled out a pink hoodie with "Destin" on the front in gold lettering.

"That really suits you," Burt said as she pulled it on over her navy SO polo.

She gave him a look. "It's Sky's."

She grabbed a white ball cap, put it on, and pulled her ponytail through it. "Do I look a little vacation-y?" she asked the guys.

"Got a fanny pack?" Dwight asked.

"Let's tease later," Wyatt said. "Maggie and I are going to wait until you guys let us know that you're in position, then we'll pull right up in front."

"Wyatt's staying in the Jeep, until it's time to roll," Maggie said.

"I was gonna say, he's kinda hard not to recognize."

A minute later, the others had moved into the cover of the empty lot. Within a few steps, they were invisible, though Maggie could hear the faint sound of brush moving. Wyatt walked over to his open window, pulled out his SO ball cap, and slapped it on.

"I hate seeing you suited up again," Maggie said.

"Why?" He tugged his vest down just a tad. "I think I look pretty hot."

"You know why," she answered. "I've gotten used to not worrying about you anymore."

"Well, you should know that I'm pretty unenthusiastic about you being here, too," he said. He took a pair of sunglasses out of his shirt pocket and slid them onto her face. "You got shot on our second date, and I got shot on our third. Now, we're getting married in a week and I think we should both go out of town till then."

"Thanks, you're making me feel a lot better," Maggie said.

"I consider it my duty."

He frowned down at her, his eyes troubled and his jaw set.

"We'll be okay," Maggie said quietly.

"Yes, we will," he answered. He gave her a light kiss. "We've already paid for the barbecued ribs."

⚓ ⚓ ⚓

A few minutes later, Maggie drove around the circular drive in front of the office. On the other side of the circle were two covered parking spaces against the side of the hotel. They were marked for handicapped guests and loading and unloading only.

There was a wall on Wyatt's side of the Jeep. It was the back of the ice room and elevator. A wheelchair ramp led up to the pool on the left side of the wall. A short set of concrete steps led up to the open hallway on the other side.

Maggie got out of the Jeep, opened her cargo door, and pulled out her overnight bag. Then she started wheeling it across the circular drive to the steps that led up to the glass-fronted office. She looked to her left to see if anyone was in the hall. There weren't any humans, but her old friend Tom sat in front of the elevator with his back to her.

She'd found Tom as a kitten, injured by the side of Bluff Road. After trying to give him to her parents and every single person she worked with, she'd gotten the former manager at Water Street to take him. Maggie used to stop by and see him when she was still on patrol, and he was now enormous and spoiled.

She turned her eyes back to the front as she took the steps, her bag thumping along behind her. Through the glass front door, she saw Linda sitting at the reception counter. As usual, she was wearing reading glasses on her nose, and glasses for distance on top of her head.

She stood up as Maggie opened the door and walked in.

"No, girl, because listen," Linda said, pointing her finger. "I know something's going on, and my pressure can't take none of this."

Maggie walked up to the desk. "It'll be okay. I just need to get into one of the first-floor rooms, so I can get a look out back from the screened porch."

"I knew he was a creep," Linda said. "I knew that already. What did he do?"

"I'll tell you later. Do you have a room on the first floor that's not occupied?"

"Yeah, one second. But I'm unhappy." Linda pecked at her computer. "106. That author lady's supposed to be checking in there, but she's not due till tonight."

"What author lady?"

"I don't know, mysteries, whatever. I don't have time to read. She comes down here a lot." She pulled a key card from a drawer and started running it through a machine. "She and Tom have some kind of thing going, and that's the only room she'll take cause Tom will stay there with her. I don't think all her tires are properly inflated, if you know what I mean. Now he sits out there all the time waitin' on her like some kind of lovesick fool."

She handed Maggie the key card and stood up. "It's by the elevator, that first room. Are you just talking to this guy or are you arresting him?"

"We're arresting him."

"We?" Linda asked.

"There's a few of us outside," Maggie said.

"I need to find a job where I can work at the house, you know what I'm saying? What do you want me to do?"

"I just want you to go in the back there and stay put," Maggie said. "I'll come back and get you in a few minutes."

"Listen to me, I'm going back there and smokin' me a cigarette cause I know this isn't good. If the boss comes in and smells smoke tomorrow, I'm telling her to call you."

"Okay," Maggie said distractedly, and she went back outside and turned right. The open hallway turned into an ell on the left to take guests to their rooms. To the right, it led to the docks.

Maggie took the left and met Tom in front of the ice room. "Hey, Tom," she said quietly, then turned the corner to room 106. Tom followed, and watched as she stood her suitcase up, then ran the card through the door. It beeped and the green light flashed. Maggie opened the door with one hand and scooped Tom up with the other. She deposited him in the hallway that ran past two bedrooms and opened into a living room/kitchen combination. At the far end were two sets of French doors that opened onto a spacious, screened balcony.

Maggie made her way to them, opened the door on the left side, and stuck her head out. The building was built in such a way that the screened balconies were staggered, affording everyone an unobstructed view of the docks and Scipio Creek.

Maggie didn't see anything at first. There were only two boats occupying the hotel's slips; a small sailboat that was moored there permanently, and a center console that looked to be empty.

She stepped out onto the balcony, just far enough to see all the way down the building. About halfway down was a man in white painter's coveralls, painting the white metal railing that ran along the outside walkway, then down a ramp to the docks.

She could only see his profile, but the square jaw and close-cropped sandy hair matched the picture in his file.

She watched a moment, as he bent over to dip his brush in the gallon of paint he'd placed on a blue tarp. When he'd painted a few strokes without looking nervous or distracted, she stepped back into the room and quietly closed the door. She pulled her hoodie off and keyed her shoulder mic.

"He's about dead center of the building, on the ramp that goes down to the docks" she said.

Wyatt's voice came back. "Burt, back up Pax and Jack. Dwight, through the pool area to that back hallway there. Maggie and I will take the hall between the rooms and the office. Take those positions and wait for my go."

Maggie slid the key card into her back pocket, pulled out her Glock, and opened the door. Wyatt was just coming around the corner, his service weapon in hand. Maggie shoved Tom back with her foot, then went out and closed the door behind her quietly.

"I'm point," Wyatt said, and Maggie didn't bother arguing.

He moved back out into the breezeway, and around the corner, Maggie on his heels. With the cover of the floor above, the hallway was like a tunnel, and a brisk breeze blew through it from the creek in back.

The two of them made their way halfway down the ramp, and Wyatt looked around a small hibiscus, at the back of the hotel. He pulled his head back and nodded at Maggie.

"Go!" he said quietly into his mic, and whipped around the corner in a crouch, Maggie right behind him.

"Curt Shook, freeze!" Wyatt yelled.

"Down, get down!" Maggie heard Pax yell before she circled Wyatt and could see the docks. Wyatt moved down to the dock itself, his gun trained on Shook, who was slowly raising his hands. White paint dripped from the brush he was still holding.

Maggie went to the left, stepping up on the walkway, aiming her weapon at Shook. Pax and Myles were in shooting stance at the other end of the dock.

"Curt Shook, lie face down on the ground," Wyatt said as he slowly advanced from one direction, and Pax did the same from the other.

Shook hesitated a moment, glaring at Wyatt. His eyes were bright green, but cold. His skin was dark and weathered.

"Face down now!" Myles yelled.

Shook slowly descended to his knees, tossed the brush aside, and laid down.

"Hands behind your back," Wyatt yelled.

Shook complied, slowly, and Wyatt and Pax moved in simultaneously. Wyatt walked closer, his gun levelled at Shook.

"Cuff him, Pax," he said.

Pax pulled the cuffs from his belt, knelt down, and secured Shook's wrist. Once he had, Maggie and the others, including Wyatt, holstered their weapons.

"What are you guys hassling me for?" Shook asked, his voice reminiscent of smoky bars.

"You're under arrest for the kidnapping and murder of Kristen Morgan," Wyatt said.

"Bull," the man said. "I never heard of her."

Pax jerked Shook to his feet.

"I think it'll come back to you shortly," Wyatt said. He looked over his shoulder at Burt, who had come to stand beside Maggie. "Burt, bring the cruiser around."

Jack followed Pax as he guided Shook along the walkway toward the front of the hotel. Wyatt and Maggie walked ahead.

Maggie jogged over to the office door and opened it. "Linda, it's all clear," she called.

"You don't need to talk to me—" Maggie heard before the door eased shut. Wyatt stood at the corner of the hallway as he watched Pax and Jack walk Shook down the steps to the circular drive.

Maggie pulled the key card from her back pocket. "I need to go get my hoodie," she said. "And Tom."

"Who's Tom?" Wyatt asked as she walked away.

CHAPTER

TWENTY

urt Shook was the kind of guy that other tough guys gave a wide berth in a bar or a pool hall. There was something about him, his expression, his body language, that probably kept him from having to put much effort into being left alone. It was an evident meanness, an obvious willingness to hurt. Right now, he was angry, and that anger, though he seemed to be trying to keep it in check, gave off waves that could almost be felt physically.

Maggie and Wyatt walked into the interview room and sat down at the table, across from Shook. Dwight had been tasked with filing the arrest report and going through Shook's personal belongings, so Burt sat in the corner by the small table that held the recording equipment.

Shook hadn't said a word since they'd read him his rights at Water Street.

"Talk to me about Kristen Morgan," Wyatt said quietly.

"Don't know her," Shook said, his face expressionless.

"She knew you," Wyatt said.

"Yeah? How's that?"

"She had your DNA under her fingernails."

Shook smiled and held up his arms as far as he could, the cuffs clinking against the side of the table. "That's crap. Not a scratch on me, man."

"You watch too much TV," Wyatt said. "She didn't have to draw blood. She just needed to scrape off a few skin cells. Your DNA is in the system from your last arrest. When you beat the crap out of your girlfriend? You remember that."

"So?" Shook asked, but he looked less sure. "Maybe I ran into her somewhere. Maybe we hooked up."

"Listen up. You're not half as smart as you think you are, and you're twice as screwed."

"How's that?"

"We have your DNA under a dead woman's fingernails, and a witness that puts you at Lake Morality at the time that dead woman was killed there."

"What witness?"

"A corrections officer from Franklin." Wyatt raised his eyebrows. "As witnesses go, law enforcement officers are our favorite."

Shook licked at the corner of his lip. His eyes narrowed, and darted around on the opposite wall, like he was trying to remember seeing someone.

"Kidnapping and first-degree murder, and you're a two-time loser," Wyatt said. "You're looking at the death penalty, Curt."

"I want my lawyer," Shook said.

"I'm sure you do," Wyatt said. "Who's your lawyer?"

Shook hesitated a moment. "I don't have one."

"So, public defender," Wyatt said. "Hey, maybe you'll get that new kid, Morrison. He seems like a good kid, but don't let him talk you into pleading not guilty. He hasn't actually tried a case yet, so he'll probably be kind of eager to get the experience. Unfortunately, it's a loser. A jury's going to take one look at your record and our evidence and vote guilty in time to be home for dinner."

Maggie watched Shook as his jaw clenched and he looked somewhere above her head. His eyes began to water, and Maggie thought he might cry. But he didn't look sad, or scared; he looked frustrated.

"Are you upset about something, Mr. Shook?" she asked him.

Shook's eyes dropped down to hers. "Is that supposed to be funny?"

Maggie felt bugs crawling on her skin. "Not at all. You look pretty pissed."

"You should see me when I'm pissed," he said quietly.

"Yeah," Maggie said, nodding slowly. "I bet Kristen could say quite a lot about that."

"You don't know anything, lady." He sat forward in his chair, and Maggie saw the veins in his neck swell.

"You people talk to me like I'm some kind of idiot. You think I'm just some loser you can push around. Some loser who doesn't have anything going for him. I'm a trained chef! Did you know that? You know what I did my last spin in Franklin? I went through the culinary arts program. I've got a certificate! You know all those pansy-ass chefs on those cooking shows on TV? I watched all those guys, and I can cook circles around every single one of 'em."

"A chef, huh?" Wyatt looked down at the file in front of him. "I don't see anything about being a chef, but I know that, as of about an hour ago, you were painting trim for fifteen bucks an hour."

Shook jerked in his chair, his cuffs straining. "Because nobody would give me a damn job!" he yelled. "Looking down their noses at me, looking at my applications like I was an idiot! Roberson's over in St. Joe, acting like they were gonna do me a favor and put me on as a dishwasher, because they try to help guys out."

He raised his hands and jabbed his finger at the air between them. "I don't need any of those people, and I don't need any favors! I'm opening my own place!"

"Is that a fact?" Wyatt asked.

"You think I'm kidding? I've got a place in Carrabelle, could be open in two-three months."

"Not anymore," Wyatt said. "Not unless you're partners with somebody who *isn't* about to go to prison."

Shook brought his hands down hard on the table, but the short leash he was on kept him from making as much impact as he probably meant to. He slammed them down again, and then again. The table jerked a bit, but Maggie and Wyatt kept their seats.

"You through?" Wyatt asked quietly.

"Let me tell you who's through," Shook said, pointing his fists at Wyatt. "He's through. He's way through."

"Who is?" Maggie asked.

Shook took a deep breath, spittle gathering at the corners of his mouth, then sat back as he blew it out. "No."

"No, what?" Wyatt asked.

"I'm not saying anything till you guarantee me no death penalty," he said. He leaned forward again. "I want it in writing that I do life without."

"I'm not the State's Attorney," Wyatt said.

"Then talk to him," Shook said as he sat back again. "I'm not talking anymore until I see it in writing. You send me down for death row, you can figure it out on your own, do your own damn jobs. You want me to help you out, you get me what I want."

Wyatt tapped his pen against the side of the table for a moment, then stood. Maggie stood with him.

"We'll get back to you," Wyatt said.

"You do that," Shook said. "Meanwhile, I need a soda. My sugar's low."

Wyatt didn't bother answering. He held the door open for Maggie, then followed her out.

"He's talking about Morgan," Maggie said.

"I'm sure he is," Wyatt said. "I'll go call the State's Attorney's office. Do me a favor and get him a Coke or something, so we don't have to listen to him whine."

⚓ ⚓ ⚓

Twenty minutes later, Wyatt and Maggie walked back into the interview room, where Shook and Burt sat waiting.

Wyatt slid a piece of paper in front of Shook. "There you go."

Wyatt and Maggie sat back down as Shook looked over the document. On State's Attorney letterhead, it stated in one paragraph that their office would not seek the death penalty for the crimes Shook would be charged with that day, contingent upon his full cooperation in apprehending anyone else who had a hand in Kristen Morgan's death. It was signed "Dwight G. Shultz," which made it meaningless, but it also made it more of a practical joke than an instrument of deceit by either the State's Attorney or the Sheriff's Office.

Shook read it over, might even have read it twice, then sat back in his chair.

"It's gonna be his own damn fault," he said, nodding. "Thinks he's so much smarter than me. I went to him for a straight-up business deal. Three times he tells me no. Like he's too good for me. Then he has to make it this big complicated thing, and put my life on the line, because he's not enough of a man to take care of his business himself."

"Who?" Wyatt asked.

"Who do you think?" Shook spat out. "Little rich boy, mister big-time finance. The husband."

"Craig Morgan," Wyatt said.

"Of course Craig Morgan," Shook said.

"Tell me how that goes," Wyatt said.

"I'll tell you how it goes," Shook said mockingly. He sat forward again, his chest up against the table. "Nobody wants to give me a commercial loan because I'm a big, bad felon. So, I took out a mortgage on my house. Sixty-thousand bucks, so I can put a down payment on this empty restaurant Morgan's selling and get it fixed up. He gives it to me, for 20k down and owner financing, but this huge monthly payment, right? Now, after all the money I put into redoing the place, the inspectors are telling me I need sprinklers inside, and a whole new ventilation system, and new ceiling tiles. They won't pass me."

He takes up his soda in both hands, takes a long drink.

"So, I try to get him to work some kinda deal with me, give me a break, cause I don't have enough money to do that stuff and pay him his monthly payments, too," Shook said. "So, after like the third time I go to him, he asks me how important it is to me. I tell him it's everything man, cause I'm gonna lose my restaurant, and the bank is gonna get my house for a lousy sixty-grand, cause I'm not making any money on a restaurant I can't open!"

"Okay," Wyatt said.

"So, he offers me a deal," Shook said. "I take care of his problem, and he writes me a new contract on the building. No payments, just five percent of what I make every month once it's open. *And* he'll pay for the improvements on the place."

"And what was his problem?" Maggie asked.

"Her. The wife," Shook answered. "I jack her and the car, dump them in the lake. Supposed to look like she did it herself. He says she's a whack job." He sat forward again. "I'm no idiot, I got the new contract before I ever even saw her. It's in my car; you can go see for yourself."

"Why?" Maggie asked.

"Why what?"

"Why did he want his wife dead?" she answered.

Shook shrugged. "He was tired of her. Said her mental problems were dragging him down, that she was gonna hurt his career. Said he was tired of everything."

"So, tell us what happened Tuesday," Wyatt said.

"It was all screwed up," Shook said. "He told me she was going to town, and I waited in that parking lot, by the bridge, till she came in. Then I followed her. First she went to the Sponge Company, downtown, but I couldn't do anything there, with people everywhere. But then she went to the park, the botanical gardens. There wasn't anybody around, so I parked in the public lot across from the Water Street Hotel, where the RVs always park. And I waited for her to come out."

"What about your car?" Wyatt asked. "If you were supposed to take her car, what about your car?"

Shook shrugged. "No big deal to ride my bike back to town in a day or so, get my car. It's a public lot, and I'm doing work at the hotel."

"Okay. So what happened when she came out?"

"She messed me up, man," Shook said. "I started walking over there when she was putting the stroller in the back. I was like, almost right there when she saw me. She was just opening her door when she looked over, and I was like ten feet from her. I had my .45. I tell her uh-uh, get in the passenger side. Chick looks at me and her eyes go all big, and before I even get there, she throws the keys inside and slams the door."

Maggie could picture that. She was pretty sure she could see Kristen's face pretty accurately, see the fear there. Maggie had been terrified more than once, and she knew the fluttering that Kristen felt in her chest, the almost nauseous feeling in her stomach. The fight or flight adrenaline that hit her like a sudden sickness. Maggie could feel those things, but they were quickly overshadowed by the anger that poured over her like a hot shower. She wanted to reach over and choke him.

"Keep talking," Wyatt said.

"Well, I'm there, right? She's already seen me, so I figure Plan B. I grab her and tell her to move it, walk her to my car."

"And she just went?"

"I had a gun, man."

"She had to think you wouldn't just shoot her in the street in broad daylight," Wyatt said.

"Yeah? I told her in for a penny, in for a pound. I've already done enough to go back in. She gives me any more trouble, tries to run, I tell her, and I walk back there and shoot her kid right through the window."

Maggie glanced over at Wyatt. His usually-warm eyes were flat and his face unreadable, at least to a casual bystander.

"So, you take her in your car? Where?"

"To my house, man. I gotta regroup, wait for him to figure out what the hell he wants to do now. I had to hang onto her all night."

"Yeah," Wyatt said. "So you doped her up and then used your cute little sex cuffs to hook her up to the bed."

Shook's eyes narrowed. "You were in my *house*?"

"Warrant and everything," Wyatt answered. "We saw your toy collection."

Just then, Dwight's face appeared in the little window. Maggie saw him, lightly slapped Wyatt's shoulder, and pointed. Wyatt looked, then got up and went out into the hall.

"What's up, Dwight?"

Dwight held up the evidence bag with Shook's cell phone in it. "This. Somebody's called him three times in like ten minutes."

"You run the number?"

"It's a burner," Dwight answered. "Local area code."

Wyatt nodded. "Okay, give it to me," he said.

Dwight put the phone in Wyatt's hand. "How's it going?"

"We hate him more than we thought we would," Wyatt said, then he opened the door, went back in the room, and pulled it shut behind him.

He sat back down, pulled the phone out of the bag. The missed call notifications were still on the screen. "Who's this?"

Shook leaned forward. "Him. Morgan."

Wyatt put the phone down between him and Maggie. "What does he want?"

"How the hell should I know? I haven't answered the phone."

"What happened when you told him things got messed up?" Wyatt asked. "I assume you guys made contact."

"Yeah. He panicked. Little rich boy can't think so fast on his feet. He told me to just wait for him to call me back. So I did."

"And?"

"He called me back in the morning, told me to still take her out to the lake. The lake was my idea. I told him it would have to be that night. So, I hung onto her till later. But when I took her out to the car, the car didn't start. Alternator's done."

"So?"

"So I borrowed somebody else's vehicle."

"Whose?" Wyatt asked.

"Nobody's. Somebody I knew from Franklin. Dumbass doesn't know anything. He was supposed to pick me up from the lake Tuesday night, but that went all to hell."

Just then, Shook's phone vibrated and the screen lit up. Maggie and Wyatt both looked at it. It was the same number.

Shook leaned over, craned his neck to see, then sat back, smiling. "You should answer it," Shook said. "He'd probably piss himself."

They let it vibrate until it stopped and the missed call notification popped onto the screen again.

"What about the baby?" Maggie asked.

"What about it?"

"Was Kristen supposed to drop her off somewhere?" Wyatt asked, putting air quotes around her name. "Is that how he was going to get the baby back?"

Shook huffed out a short, dry laugh. "Back? There was no 'back'. It was supposed to be her, the baby, and the car, all of 'em in the lake."

Shook's tight smile made Maggie feel sick. She looked over at Wyatt, who opened his mouth to say something, but they were interrupted by the muffled ring of Maggie's phone. She pulled it out and was about to decline the call when she saw the number. She turned it so Wyatt could see. It was the same number that had been calling Shook.

She and Wyatt both stood up as it rang for the third time and got out into the hall by the fourth ring. Maggie walked briskly down the hall as she answered, Wyatt on her heels.

"This is Maggie Redmond," she said.

"Lt. Redmond," Morgan said. "This is Craig Morgan."

"Hello, Craig, how are you?"

Maggie rounded the corner to the lobby and headed for the receptionist's desk.

"Uh, I'm fine, thank you," Morgan said, but he didn't sound so fine. "I, uh, I was wondering if you had any news."

"No, I'm sorry," Maggie said as she and Wyatt reached the front desk. Louann looked up at them expectantly. "I've been in court all day. In fact, the break's over and I'll need to go back in in just a minute."

Wyatt grabbed a pad from Louann's desk and started scribbling.

"Please let me assure you, though, Mr. Morgan," Maggie continued. "Your wife is still my top priority. We're working on another angle. We'll see if it gets us anywhere."

She read the note as Wyatt spun it around for Louann. It told her that if anyone called, Maggie was in court for the day.

"What new angle?" Morgan was asking.

"Well, because of Kristen's history, the times she, uh, got into some trouble with other men, we're running down guys with violent histories, especially sexual violence, that she might have crossed paths with."

"But, I don't understand," Morgan said. "You didn't say anything about Kristen being...violated."

"She wasn't," Maggie said as she turned around and started walking back up the hall. Wyatt followed. "But she might have run into the wrong guy, a guy that didn't accept 'no' for an answer. It might have escalated, and he killed her."

Morgan was silent for a moment. Maggie and Wyatt stopped at the door to the interview room.

"Mr. Morgan?" Maggie prompted. "I'm sorry, I know that's a very unpleasant thought."

"Uh, yes. Yes," Morgan said. He sounded distracted.

"Mr. Morgan, I'm sorry, but I need to go back into the courtroom. I'll give you a call tomorrow and let you know how the investigation is going, okay?"

"Sure. Yes," he said. "Thank you."

He hung up, and Maggie looked up at Wyatt. "He's so rattled he called me on the wrong phone."

"He doesn't like that he can't get hold of Shook," Wyatt said, frowning.

"He might be scared enough to bolt," Maggie said.

"Maybe. But, maybe you just bought us some time. I believed you, and I'm standing right here."

"It's not going to be enough. Not for long."

"No."

"We need to get him in custody today," Maggie said firmly. "Today."

"Yes, but we need to get him out of that house," Wyatt said. "We're not going in there with the baby and two, three other people there."

"No."

Wyatt looked over Maggie's shoulder, and she turned around. Louann had popped her head around the corner.

"Some man just called for you," she said. "I told him you had court all day."

"Did he give you his name?" Maggie asked.

"No, he just said he'd call back and hung up on me."

Maggie nodded. "Okay."

Louann disappeared, and Maggie turned around to face Wyatt.

"We've gotta get him out of the house," she said.

They stood there for a moment, Wyatt with his hand on the door knob.

"I think I have something," Wyatt said finally.

⚓ ⚓ ⚓

Craig Morgan was sitting out on the back patio, staring at the hedges that made up the border of his back yard, and trying to get a grip. The last thing he needed to do was to panic and screw up something that wasn't already screwed up. The fact that he couldn't get Shook to answer the phone was upsetting, but it didn't mean the cops had found out about him somehow. Maybe he'd gone out and left his phone at home. Maybe he was asleep.

Kate was inside napping, and his sister was sitting with Ellie on a crib blanket in the grass. The baby had been cranky all day, and Miranda was trying to appease her with some stuffed toys.

His head jerked around when his own cell phone rang from the glass table beside him. He didn't recognize the number, but it was local. He considered not answering but, picked up on the third ring.

"Hello?"

"Hello, is this Mr. Craig Morgan?" an older man asked.

"Who's this, please?" Craig answered.

"I'm sorry," the man said politely. "This is Dr. Larry Davenport, the Franklin County Medical Examiner."

Morgan's heart started pounding. "Yes?"

"First of all, please accept my sincere condolences on the loss of your wife," Davenport said. He sounded old as dirt.

"Uh, thank you," Morgan said.

"I'm sorry to trouble you, but Wesley Crematorium called and they said they were ready to pick up your wife's remains."

"They said they were faxing you the paperwork yesterday," Morgan said.

"Yes, and they did, thank you," Davenport said. "But I'm afraid you'll need to sign the release form, giving us permission to release her to them."

Morgan thought a minute. "Uh, now's not a very good time," he said. "Can you fax it to me?"

"No, I'm sorry. The law requires that you sign in person, and show your ID, before we can relinquish her remains." The man sighed. "I'm sorry for the imposition, but there have been…well, instances where family members didn't agree on disposition of the body and tried to make their own arrangements. Or even, I'm sad to say, when the deceased have been taken by strangers, for reasons I won't go into."

Morgan licked his lips and thought a minute. "So, you're, uh, you're done with Kristen's, uh, body?"

"Yes. I'm afraid your wife has told us all she can."

"Okay. Uh, does it need to be right now?"

"Please. They said they'll be picking her up by four."

"Okay, well. It'll take me just a bit," Morgan said.

"That's fine," Davenport said. "Do you know where Weems Memorial Hospital is?"

"Yes."

"The morgue—my office, is located at the back. If you'll just press the button at the back door, someone will admit you."

"Okay, thank you," Morgan said.

"Thank you, sir," Davenport said, and hung up the phone.

Morgan tapped the phone against his leg as he watched his sister bouncing a little purple elephant around on the blanket, making stupid little noises that apparently didn't impress Ellie much.

Morgan rubbed at his neck, trying to work out the tension that had been there for days, making his muscles tight and giving him insane headaches.

He rolled his head a few times, listening to tiny little cracking noises in his neck as he did. Then he looked back over at Ellie as she began to cry.

TWENTY-ONE

There were five law enforcement officers stationed at the back of Weems Memorial. Maggie and Dwight were in Dwight's minivan, parked in one of the handicapped spots close to the door. Wyatt had exchanged his navy polo for one of his Hawaiian shirts, and was sitting at a concrete break table under a huge old oak tree with two PD officers, one male, one female, who were wearing scrubs borrowed from Weems staffers.

One of the female deputies, wearing a bathrobe, was sitting under the portico in a wheelchair, an IV pole at her side. Everyone who was visible was wearing their body armor under their clothing.

Out front, just in case Morgan couldn't follow directions, were four more officers, two from PD and two from the SO. They were similarly trying to blend in.

Maggie watched Wyatt smile at something the female officer was saying, then pick up his cell phone. A second later, her cell rang.

"Hey," Maggie said.

"Hey. You guys good?"

"Yeah, we're fine. I wish he'd hurry up, though. I want to get this over with. This needs to be the last day that Morgan gets to use his own bathroom, you know?"

"I know. Just remember that you can't shoot him without cause," Wyatt said. "So, unless he says something mean to you, hold your fire."

"Ha-ha," Maggie said without humor.

Wyatt hung up, and Maggie put her phone back on the console.

"Y'all are gonna have a real entertaining life together," Dwight said.

"Yeah, he's a real riot."

⚓ ⚓ ⚓

"Are you sure you want to take her with you?" Miranda asked.

"Yeah, sis," Morgan answered as she finished buttoning Ellie's sweater. "I'm just not really comfortable being separated from her yet, you know what I mean?"

Miranda looked up at him sympathetically as she picked Ellie up from the living room rug. "I understand," she said. "Do you want me to go with you, though? She's been pretty fussy. I think her gums are bothering her."

"No, it's okay," Morgan said. "You stay here in case Kate needs you." He watched her put Ellie into her car seat. "I don't think she should be alone."

"I feel so bad for her," Miranda said, buckling the baby. "Her only child, you know?"

"Yeah," Morgan said.

He reached over to one of the living room chairs to pick up the purple baby carrier that Kristen had gotten at the baby shower. She liked carrying Ellie around on her chest while she cleaned the house.

"Hey, though," Morgan said. "Do you mind if I take your car, since the car seat base is already in there?"

"Yeah, sure," she answered. "The keys are hanging by the door."

"Thanks." He started buckling the carrier straps around his waist, the carrier itself hanging upside down. "I'm going to go ahead and put this on so I don't have to fool with it at the hospital. It's kind of a pain."

Miranda gave him a small smile as she stood. "You want some help?"

"I got it, thanks."

He snapped the second buckle, pulled the carrier upright, and slid the straps over his shoulders.

"I went ahead and made her a fresh bottle," Miranda said. "It's in the inside pocket of her diaper bag.

"Thanks." Morgan picked up the diaper bag, slung it onto his shoulder, then walked over to the baby in her car seat.

"You want some help out to the car?"

"No, I'm good." He leaned over and picked up the car seat. "I shouldn't be long. Just need to sign the paperwork, then I'll be right back."

"Okay," Miranda said, watching him walk down the hall. "I'm making pork loin for dinner."

"Sounds good," he said over his shoulder. "Back soon."

Morgan grabbed the keys from the hook by the door, then went out and closed the door behind him. Ellie started grumbling a little bit as he carried her to Miranda's Forrester. "Gimme a minute," he mumbled as he fingered the unlock button and opened the back door.

He dropped the diaper bag on the concrete, then lifted the car seat and plopped it facing backwards onto the base. It wobbled, then wouldn't latch when he tried to straighten it. He fumbled with it a minute, but it wouldn't go in. Ellie was screwing up her face, and he huffed out a breath and tried again. The car seat was new, and he'd only done it once before.

The car seat still wouldn't lock in place, and he cursed under his breath, then looked over his shoulder. The SUV was parked on the left side of the driveway and wasn't visible from the front windows. He looked at the car seat, thought about it for a second, then just put the car seat on the floorboard.

Then he got into the driver's seat, started the car, and drove away.

Maggie looked at her watch. "I wish he'd hurry up," she said.

Dwight looked over at her. "It's only been about thirty minutes since Larry called him."

"I know. I just want to get this over with."

She shifted in her seat, then looked out at the parking lot. "I wonder what's going to happen to Ellie after we nail this guy."

"Maybe the sister. Or the mom," Dwight said.

"Maybe. Poor little thing."

Pax's voice sounded in her ear. "Hey, you guys?"

"Yeah, Pax."

"Okay, this guy just showed up, and he looked like your description, but he wasn't driving a BMW or an Escalade, so we didn't think much about him, plus he has a baby with him. We let him go in, but once he was closer, he looked enough like your guy that I thought I should tell you."

Maggie felt something grab at her chest. "He had a baby with him?" she asked.

"Yeah, like on him," Pax said. "On his chest. You know, one of those carrier things."

"Crap. Stand by," Maggie said.

"I heard," Wyatt's voice said over the radio. "Maggie, call Larry, see if Rose can keep him in the waiting area while we regroup. I don't want him behind closed doors."

"Copy," Maggie said, and picked up her phone. She redialed Larry, and he picked up on the first ring.

"Yes, Maggie?"

"Larry, we have a problem. He's in the building, went in front. He's got the baby with him."

"Oh, that's not good," Larry said.

"Ask Rose to try to keep him in the—"

"Wherever you'd like to eat is fine, dear," Larry said, his voice a bit louder. "But I need to run; there's a family member here to see me. I'll be home soon."

Maggie started to say something, then she heard Larry speak again, not directly into the phone, but close enough.

"I'm sorry to meet you under such sad circumstances, Mr. Morgan," Larry said.

Maggie lowered her phone and looked at Dwight.

"Thank you," they heard Morgan say.

Maggie hit the mute button on her phone and shoved open her car door.

⚓   ⚓   ⚓

"Please, take a seat," Larry said, and waved a hand toward one of the two green leather armchairs in front of his desk.

Morgan sat down, adjusting the baby carrier on his lap and bouncing his leg. Ellie had started fussing out in the hallway and was screwing up her face for a good cry.

"Your daughter is lovely," Larry said, as he sat down. "I do miss that age. Even my grandchildren are grown."

Morgan nodded distractedly as Larry opened a file on his desk. Ellie let out first a hesitant squawk, then rolled that into a full-on wail.

Larry slowly flipped through some papers in the file. His hand shook, but he looked to be about a hundred years old.

"Where are my glasses?" the old man said, patting the shirt pocket he'd just put his phone in. "Ah, there we go." He picked the glasses up from his desk and put them on, then looked over them to the papers in front of him. "Oh, forgive me. This is the wrong file."

Larry eased himself up out of his chair and walked over to a credenza covered in files, books, and papers. "Here we are."

Ellie screamed into Morgan's ear and he just managed not to scream right back into her face. He hopped up and bounced up and down a few times, as the old man brought the file over to the end of his desk, opened it, and lifted out a couple of papers stapled together.

"Terribly sorry. Here you go, if you don't mind," he said, placing the papers down on the desk. Teething, I'll bet," he said, as Morgan moved back to the desk. "I well remember those days. I got more sleep in boot camp than I did while our son cut his first teeth."

"I'm sure," Morgan said, irritated. He leaned over the paperwork, and Ellie screamed louder as she leaned with him. He bounced her with one hand on her butt as he picked up the pen lying nearby,

"Would you like me to take her?" Davenport asked, smiling. "I'm quite good with babies now that I'm old."

"No, that's okay, she's fine," Morgan said as he tried to hold the paper down with the heel of his hand so he could sign.

"Oh, let me have a go at her," Larry said, and he reached over and slipped his hands under Ellie's shoulders.

"No! We're good—" Morgan started, but Larry was already lifting her up and out. "Please."

"Oh, she's a pretty girl, yes," Larry cooed. "And she smells so good. There's nothing like the smell of a baby's head, is there?"

Morgan opened his mouth to say something, he didn't know what, but the office door slammed open, and Lt. Redmond was crouched in the doorway, pointing an automatic of some kind at him. One second later, a tall guy with a moustache was standing over her, doing the same. Both of them glanced for a microsecond at the old man, then looked back at him.

"Don't move, Mr. Morgan," Maggie said.

He looked over at the old man, who was starting to back away, one hand on Ellie's butt, the other big hand covering the back of her head. Almost without thinking, he lunged for the baby.

He had just registered a huge pressure on his right knee when he heard something that sounded, to him, like a car crash. Then he was down on the floor. At first, he thought Ellie was screaming, but then he realized it was actually him, as he looked down at the leg that was sprawled outward on the floor. His leg was on fire, but he had trouble at first, connecting it to the searing heat he was feeling in his knee, or the blood that was starting to spread out around it.

He bent to grab at his leg, but the big guy pushed him in the chest with his foot, and he fell onto his back. When he looked up, Maggie Redmond was standing over him, her gun still in her hand.

"Thank you for that opportunity," she said, so quietly he almost didn't hear her.

TWENTY-TWO

Riverfront Park was empty and quiet, despite the warm, sunny weather. It was early on a Sunday morning. The shops and most of the restaurants had not yet opened and, for the most part, the tourists were sleeping in. As Maggie got out of her Jeep, a fifty-ish man wearing running gear and headphones breezed past, his athletic shoes making the barest, hollow thump on the asphalt.

Maggie shoved her purse onto the floorboard, put her phone in the pocket of her shorts, and locked and closed her door. As she walked across the grass toward the dock, the sharp *brrring brrring* of a bicycle bell sounded. An older couple glided by on a pair of the pastel-colored, vintage bicycles that were available for rent. Maggie smiled in reply, then turned back to the dock.

Two shrimp boats were docked at the park, as they frequently were, usually when they had a load to deliver to 13 Mile Seafood next to the park. When Maggie got to the dock, it was quiet enough for her to hear their fenders bumping gently against the pilings, and to pick up the slight creaking of the old wooden trawlers.

Maggie turned and headed toward the south end of the park, not more than a hundred feet away. Her destination was the waist-high wooden wall that separated the park from the house on the next lot. She'd been back to the park many times since David's death, though it took her months to be able to. The darkest day in her life had stolen one of her favorite places from her, and she had fought hard to reclaim it. But, she had never quite managed to go back to the exact spot where she had watched her husband die.

"Lt. Redmond?"

Maggie looked to her right and was surprised to see Kate Newell walking toward her across the grass. Behind her, with the front passenger door standing open, was Miranda Cookson's Chrysler. Miranda sat in the driver's seat.

"Mrs. Newell," Maggie said.

"I thought that was you," the other woman said. "I'm so glad."

Maggie waited for the woman to reach her. As she did, she noted the smudges of gray beneath her eyes, and thought perhaps there were more lines around her mouth than there had been the first time they'd met.

"I'm leaving. Well, Ellie and I," Kate said. We were just looking for a restaurant that's supposed to be here, to get some breakfast, and I saw you."

"Which restaurant?" Maggie asked her.

"Caroline's."

Maggie smiled and pointed south. "It's actually part of the Riverview Inn, right down the block," she said. "You can't miss it, it's purple."

"Oh, no wonder," Kate said. They were silent for a moment, as Maggie looked at Kate and Kate looked past her to the river.

"Ellie's coming to live with you?" Maggie asked finally.

"Yes," Kate answered. "Miranda loves Ellie, but she doesn't want children of her own, and...well, I don't know if I could give her up anyway. I told her we'll keep in touch, though. Visit."

Kate fell silent for a moment and fiddled with one of the mother of pearl buttons on her pale blue cardigan sweater.

"How old is your daughter, Lt. Redmond?"

"Maggie," Maggie said. "She just turned eighteen."

Kate gave her a partial smile, the corners of her mouth twitching, but she was looking out at the water, not at Maggie.

"Eighteen," she said. "Such a scary time, knowing that your child is about to go out into the world without you. Knowing that you won't be able to protect them from everything out there." She looked at Maggie then. "Of course, in the back of your mind, you know that this was true even when they were still at home."

Maggie nodded.

"I imagine you know that better than many mothers," Kate said quietly.

That was probably true, but Maggie just smiled in answer.

"I don't remember...I don't know if I told you, but Kristen was my only child," Kate said. "My husband died when she was just four, and we never had another child. And I never remarried." She took a deep breath and let it out, shakily. "Kristen was just...enough."

Maggie felt a warmth seep into her eyes, and she blinked it away. "I'm glad you'll have Ellie," she said. "And that she has you. You'll help each other to heal."

Kate gave her a weak smile, then looked over her shoulder at the car. Then she looked back at Maggie and took her hand. Kate's hand was much cooler than Maggie's own.

"Thank you," Kate said. "For everything you did for my daughter."

Maggie didn't think *you're welcome* was appropriate, so she just squeezed the older woman's hand. Kate squeezed back, then let go.

"Well, I have to go," she said. "Goodbye, Maggie."

"Goodbye, Kate."

She watched as Kate started back across the grass, then stopped and turned around. "I'll be praying for you," she called.

Maggie smiled and watched her get back in the car. She watched them drive away toward Caroline's, then she walked over to the wall and stood looking out at the water.

She thought about Kate and Kristen, and herself and Sky, and an old folk song came to mind. David used to sing it quite often, and Maggie had a CD with Alison Krauss's version.

As she looked out at the water, the words of the song glided through her mind. *Oh, mothers, let's go down, come on down, don't you want to go down...come on mothers, let's go down, down in the river to pray.*

The familiar and comforting sound of diesel engines drifted into her consciousness, and she watched a shrimp boat coming in, headed back from a long night on the Gulf.

Maggie closed her eyes and listened a moment. When she opened them, the trawler was directly in front of her, its wake splashing gently against the pilings below, and Maggie could see another trawler in her mind, an elderly Jefferson with peeling blue paint.

She saw David standing on deck, smiling at her as he went past. But, for the first time in almost a year, she didn't hear the thump of the explosion, didn't see the fireball that wrapped itself around the man she'd loved since they were children.

Maggie watched the white shrimp boat move past her, several gulls crisscrossing behind it, a handful of pelicans hang-gliding above.

She took in a big lungful of briny, damp air. Maybe one day, she wouldn't see Kristen Morgan thrashing underneath the water, her hands grasping for anything that could save her, her eyes bulging with fear.

Maybe one day, Kate Newell wouldn't see that, either. She hoped so.

⚓　⚓　⚓

It was an exceptionally beautiful day.

The air was warm, with just enough breeze to keep it from being too much so, and there were only a few clouds in the sky. There were several boats out on the bay behind the Redmond home, from small aluminum flat bottoms to pleasure boats with flybridges, out for a good day of fishing.

William and Robert, without much effort expended, had talked Georgia into letting them wire flowers into her ivy-covered , arched trellis, and the preacher who had baptized not only Maggie, but also her children, waited patiently underneath it.

John Solomon, who had retired from the Sheriff's Office to direct the Chamber of Commerce, was standing in front of the huge smoker that he used in his many cooking competitions, gently basting racks of pork ribs with his secret sauce.

Three long tables draped with white were arranged underneath a tent borrowed from the Elks Club. On them were platters and Tupperware containers loaded with salads, homemade rolls, side dishes and at least seven kinds of devilled eggs.

Kirk Lynch, his beautiful wife, Faith, and their little boy Hendrix were manning a smaller version of the Big Sexy Machine. No one had asked Kirk to bring it; he'd shown up with it, stating that since the wedding wasn't starting until one, Maggie was bound to ruin it at 2:50 if she didn't have her Hurricane. He claimed he really didn't care, but he wasn't in the mood to take the blame for it.

Wyatt stood on the back deck, wearing dress pants and his favorite Hawaiian shirt, pale green with pineapples on it. Next to him stood his best man, Evan Caldwell. They'd worked together for years back in Cocoa Beach, and Evan was now the Sheriff one county over. He didn't understand what casual wedding meant, and was wearing an immaculate black suit, and a shockingly white shirt. He'd taken off the tie.

Gray and Georgia were herding the guests over to stand near their backyard altar. Sky and Kyle were already there, looking as proud as if the wedding had been their idea.

Wyatt looked over at Evan. "I'll be right back."

"Then I'm grabbing another cigarette," Evan said.

Wyatt slipped through the sliding glass door and had loped halfway down the hall when Maggie rushed out of the master bedroom and stopped short. She was wearing a cream, floral skirt and a cream silk camisole. She and Wyatt were both as formal as they cared to get. He smiled at her.

"You look great," he said.

"Yeah?"

"Yeah," He walked over to her and cupped her face, gave her a kiss. "You look amazing."

"Thank you," she said, smiling up at him nervously.

"But let's hurry up and get married," he said, grabbing her hand. "Cause I'm starving."

Wyatt led Maggie outside, to cheerful applause, and they both blushed as they made their way to the front of the gathering, Evan right behind them. Georgia met them, and came to stand beside Maggie as her matron of honor.

As the pastor began to speak, Maggie looked around her, at the people they had wanted to share in this day. People she worked with every day, like Dwight, standing next to his wife, Amy, with his four-year-old on his left hip and his two year-old on his right.

People she had grown up with, and people she had known for a good long time, like Linda, who was already crying. William whipped out a handkerchief with a flourish and handed it to her.

Maggie looked at her children; Sky holding Wyatt's ring and Kyle holding Maggie's, and she looked at her father, who was looking back at her.

She swallowed hard and gave him a smile, felt her eyes water, and wished this wasn't one of the very rare days when she had decided to put on a little mascara.

Suddenly, she realized that Wyatt was saying "I do," and she turned to the pastor, listened for her part, and managed to say she did, too. Then everyone was clapping, and Wyatt was kissing her, and the world she was standing in was a happy and a safe one, a place where only good people lived and no one was trying to hurt anyone else.

As she and Wyatt walked through the little crowd of friends and family, Maggie caught a glimpse of the bay, sparkling like it had gotten all dressed up, just for them.

And out on the bay, hundreds of yards across the water, a beautifully restored 1947 Chris Craft Express Cruiser bobbed in the gentle wake of a passing cuddy. Bennett Boudreaux leaned back against the captain's seat, and though he could no longer make out the form of his daughter in the crowd, he lifted his champagne flute anyway, smiled, and took a sip.

A FEW WORDS OF
THANKS

Thank you for spending some time with these characters, and this place, that I love so much.

If you'd like to be the first to know about the next book in the series, other new releases, or events and appearances, please sign up for my newsletter, *UnForgotten*, at

DAWNLEEMCKENNA.COM

You can also hang out with myself and other readers on the Dawn Lee McKenna Facebook page. We have a lot of fun over there.

If you've missed any of the books in this series, my first book, See You, or the books in the new spin-off series about Wyatt's friend Evan Caldwell, you can find them right here.

AMAZON.COM/DAWN-LEE-MCKENNA/E/B00RC14PPG/

I'd like to thank all of the real people in Apalach who, generously and with good humor, have allowed me to turn them into fictional characters. Many thanks to John Solomon, Linda Joseph, Kirk and Faith Lynch, Chase Richards (otherwise known as Richard Chase), and Officer Shawn Chisolm, as well as to Mayor Van Johnson, Sheriff AJ Smith, the Apalachicola Police Department, and the Franklin County Sheriff's Office. All of you make these books something I could not make them on my own.

As always, so much gratitude to God, to my family, and to my friends, who put up with me so that I can write, and last but not least, to the most amazing readers any writer could hope to find. I love you all.

Made in the USA
San Bernardino, CA
03 May 2018